MACCHIATOS, MACARONS, AND MALICE

A Cape Bay Cafe Mystery Book 9

HARPER LIN

Macchiatos, Macarons, and Malice

ISBN: 978-1-987859-66-9

www.harperlin.com

Chapter 1

I WAS in my makeshift office in the back of the café, surrounded by stacks of paper that I needed to organize.

Sammy, my second-in-command, had been faux-casually mentioning to me for weeks now that maybe I wanted to clean them up or at least straighten them, but I was afraid that a piece of paper might get misplaced. At least right now I knew where everything was. Well, almost everything.

"Where is that?" I muttered to myself, flipping through the pile of papers on one corner of the desk. Not finding it, I started searching one of the other stacks.

"You need me to get that?" My beloved boyfriend, Matt, stuck his head through the doorway.

"Get what?"

"Your timer's going off."

Sure enough, it was. I don't know how I'd missed the high-pitched beeping. "Shoot! Yes, please. Thank you!"

"Put the next tray in?"

"Yes." I moved to another pile, still looking for that one sheet I needed.

"Do these need to go on the cooling rack or stay on the tray?"

Poor Matt had learned more about baking in the past few weeks helping me out in the evenings at the café than I think he'd ever dreamed. A couple weeks ago, he probably didn't even know that a cooling rack existed.

"On the tray for two minutes, and then transfer them to the cooling rack."

"Got it!"

There seemed to be an awful lot of banging coming from his direction, but I didn't see how it could go too horribly wrong. They were just cookies. Cookies I needed for Mrs. D'Angelo's Ladies' Auxiliary meeting I was catering, but still just cookies. Of course, I would never hear the end of it if everything wasn't perfect. Mrs. D'Angelo wasn't the type of person to just let that kind of thing roll off her back. She wasn't the type of person to let it stop her from ordering from me again either.

Matt's head popped in again. "How much time on the timer?"

"Nine minutes," I answered without looking up. I

still hadn't found the one sheet of paper I was looking for, and now I couldn't even remember which piles I'd already looked through.

Matt disappeared again for a few seconds to set the timer then came back. "What are you looking for?"

"The quote for the gelato freezers." I went back to another pile that I was pretty sure I'd already checked, but maybe I'd just missed it somehow.

"You mean this?" Matt slid a piece of paper out from under my elbow and held it up.

"Yes, that! Thanks." I took it from him and set it down on the keyboard to look over it yet again.

The freezer was pricey, but I was optimistic that it was worth it. Our traffic during the summer months was already high, but I felt like we were missing out on the opportunity to get more families in the door. Mom and Dad might like a good cup of coffee, but did they want to wait in line for it when the kids wanted ice cream? If I could have more offerings that appealed to the whole family, I could really increase my business. But I needed solid numbers to go over with my accountant before I could do anything.

I ran my finger down the quote then plugged the numbers into the spreadsheet already on my screen and checked the adjusted calculations. I felt like the numbers were too conservative. What if I...

Matt pulled a chair up next to me and swung it around to sit backward, his arms resting over the back. He looked like the cool teacher all the kids loved in a nineties sitcom or high school movie. A backward baseball cap would really sell it, but unfortunately, he hadn't brought one.

"Franny."

"Hmm?" I adjusted the numbers again. Maybe I needed separate columns for the different risk profiles. Or a whole separate worksheet.

"Look at me."

I held up a finger. "Just one second." Something wasn't adding up right. There was no way the profit estimation should be this low.

"Franny," he said again. This time, he reached out and grabbed my arm, pulling my hand off the keyboard. I looked at him, if only because it didn't actually do much good to stare at my spreadsheet if I couldn't adjust it. "Other hand." He wagged his free hand at me, his reach limited by the chair back. He would have been able to reach my other hand if he hadn't been trying to show what a cool, approachable teacher he was. Still, I gave him my other hand. I did like him after all. He tugged at it. "Face me."

"I am."

"No, really, turn your whole body and face me."

I turned sideways in the chair. The sooner I humored him and did what he said, the sooner I could get back to work.

He held both my hands in his and looked into my eyes. I'll admit, it could have been romantic, the two of us alone in the café, holding hands, gazing into each other's eyes with the smell of fresh-baked cookies wafting through the air—

"Did you move those cookies to the cooling rack?"

"No, I'll do it in a minute. I want to talk to you."

I pulled my hand away and started to push myself up. "They need to be moved to the cooling rack. The pans are still hot, and the cookies will be overcooked if they don't get moved over. And you know how Mrs. D'Angelo is about everything being perfect."

Cool Mr. Cardosi stood up in the awkward way one had to when sitting backward on a chair. "I'll do it. If you go, you'll get distracted and never come back."

As soon as he was out of the room, I turned back to my spreadsheet even though I knew it only took a second to transfer the cookies. If I could just figure out what was wrong with the numbers…

Matt came back and sat down again, instantly transforming back into Mr. Cardosi. I would have had a crush on him if I were one of his students.

"Franny," he said yet again, prompting me to turn around and let him take my hands. His warm brown eyes smiled into mine. Yes, I would have had a big crush on him. "What do you say we get out of town for a couple days? Get a room at a nice place up in the Berkshires with good room service and a fancy spa? Spend a couple of days alone together, just you and me? What do you say?"

At any other time, it would have sounded lovely, but I was so busy with the café this time of year, getting everything geared up for the summer tourist season.

Antonia's Italian Café had been a staple of family vacations in Cape Bay for almost seventy-five years. Multiple generations of families had come through our doors. Grandparents would come in carrying their little grandchildren and reminisce about the days when I was as small as their grandbaby, when they would come in with their children who were now grown and watch as my mother toted me around on her hip as she delivered the coffee and food my grandparents made behind the counter. Summer was our most important time, not just for our bottom line but for the people who considered a visit or five a family tradition.

"Matty," I started, slipping, as I often did, into using the nickname I'd called him when he was just my buddy from two doors down. "You know I would love to, but the café—"

"The café will be here when you get back."

"I know, but it's such a busy time of year—"

"It's only going to get busier."

"But there's so much that needs to be done. There's the gelato freezer and scheduling musicians so we can start having live music nights and hiring new staff and looking into expanding—"

Matt let go of my hands and propped his elbows

on the chair back so he could press the heels of his hands into his eye sockets. His sigh gave away his frustration. I felt bad, but what could I do?

"Franny, all those things can wait."

"I'm sorry. Maybe after the season is over, we can do something."

He dropped his hands in front of him. "You want me to wait six months to spend time with my girlfriend?"

"We spend time together. We spend lots of time together! We're spending time together now."

He looked at me with puppy dog eyes. "You call this spending time together? I rotate your pans in and out of the oven while you work in here, shuffling papers around and fiddling with a spreadsheet?"

"At least we're together."

"When was the last time we went out for a romantic dinner? A movie? A walk on the beach? When was the last time we sat on the couch together without you falling asleep? When was the last time you spent more than a few hours away from the café?" I started to answer the last one, but he held up his hand. "Without thinking about it or talking about it or practicing a recipe for it or working on a new plan for it? You've been working until ten or eleven o'clock every night for weeks now. If I want to see you, I have to come here and help you bake. If this is what it's like now, what's it going to be like this summer, when the café opens earlier and closes later?

I hardly see you anymore. Latte probably thinks he lives with me now."

Latte, my sweet latte-colored Berger Picard dog. "That's not fair. I spend a lot of time with him! We go for a long walk every morning."

"Do you?"

I thought for a moment and realized he was right. Matt had started taking Latte running with him every morning, and since he was already getting that exercise, we hadn't been going on our walks as much. In fact, I couldn't remember the last time we had. I hadn't really thought about how that must seem to Latte. I'd just been grateful that he was getting his exercise and I could use the time we normally spent walking to come into the café a little earlier to get some of the business stuff done before I had to work the counter.

I didn't say anything, but Matt knew my answer. "No. You're always here. You're always baking or planning some new thing you want to start doing. Even when you're not here, you're thinking about it. You even talk about it in your sleep."

As far as I knew, I had never talked in my sleep, but so what if I did, and so what if it was about Antonia's?

"Matt, the café is my life. You know that. It's my heritage, my legacy. It's my future. This place is everything to me."

He looked at me for a long time. "And what am I, Franny?"

Despite the heat from the oven that had been running all day, I felt cold. I didn't know what to say. Of course he was important to me. I loved him. I adored him! I wasn't intentionally neglecting him. Things at the café were just really busy right now. I was gearing up for the first summer season I would be running the café all on my own. I needed to make sure everything was perfect so that everyone would know that nothing had changed now that the café had passed on to the third generation of the Amaro family.

Matt nodded and stood up. He swung his leg around the chair and stepped back toward the door in one smooth motion.

"No, Matt, wait!" I jumped from my chair and climbed over his to get to him and take both his hands in mine. "I'm sorry. You're right. I'm spending too much time here and not enough time with you. I—I let myself get overwhelmed with all the things I feel like I can and should do around here, and I just took for granted that you'd still be there when I got to the other side of it all. Everything doesn't have to be perfect. No one will care if I don't have a face painter."

"A face painter?"

"Yeah, I was thinking about getting a face painter

in once a week for the kids. They love that kind of thing, you know?"

Matt shook his head slowly, but I caught the faintest twinkle in his eye. "You're too much. You know that?"

"Yeah, I know." I smiled up at him, and he bent his head to brush his lips across mine.

"So you want to go away with me? I found a gorgeous place up in the Berkshires. They have a huge spa and a world-class golf course."

I wrinkled my nose. "Golf?"

He smiled, his eyes in a full-on twinkle now. "Okay, maybe no golf this time. But they have a French bakery too. Some big-name chef I've never heard of."

"Not Jacques de Gaulle!"

"That's the one."

I swooned dramatically in his arms. "I've always wanted to try his food. His macarons are supposed to be divine. Like angels dancing on your tongue."

He chuckled. "Well, you can find out this weekend."

"This weekend?" The thought of leaving so soon had me panicking a little, but I tried to suppress it for him.

"Yes, we leave tomorrow and come back Monday."

"But that's—Friday, Saturday, Sunday, Monday—that's four days!"

He shrugged. "Two whole days and two halves."

I swallowed hard. That was a lot of time to be away from the café and not a lot of time to prepare for it.

An eyebrow went up. "Is that a problem?"

I took a deep breath. "Nope. It sounds perfect."

"Perfect."

His head bent down again, but this time wasn't just a brush of his lips. It was a long, slow, deep kiss that was just like the long weekend would be—perfect.

Chapter 2

THE HOTEL WAS stunning from the moment we turned into the long, curvy, tree-lined driveway. Rolling hills and lush forests were the furthest thing I could imagine from the beaches of Cape Bay.

"Pretty, huh?" Matt asked as we rounded yet another curve and caught a glimpse of the stunning landscape of the valley below.

"It's amazing."

And I was amazed again when we turned one final corner and the hotel came into view. "That's the hotel?"

"That's it."

He'd told me before we left that we were going to the Alford Inn, but I'd never heard of it and had been too busy getting everything sorted out at the café to look it up before we left. And then Matt and I were talking the whole four-hour car ride across Massachusetts, and I just hadn't thought to do it. In my head, I'd pictured a cozy little place, maybe a bed and breakfast or a small boutique hotel. Maybe we'd be there with just a handful of other couples. After all, that was what an inn was, wasn't it? The fact that it had a spa, a golf course, and a fancy French bakery didn't mean it couldn't be small, right?

Not this place. No, this place wasn't a little house tucked into the hills. This was a Gilded Age mansion, complete with towers and turrets and spires and balconies. It looked like something from *The Great Gatsby*. It was stunning.

"Are you sure we're in the right place?"

"I'm sure." The corner of Matt's mouth tweaked up as he pulled up into the circular driveway and stopped in front of the house. Two valets instantly appeared on either side of us to open our doors. The one on my side even offered his hand to help me out of the car.

"Checking in, sir?" the valet on Matt's side asked.

"Yes, we are."

"Excellent." He pulled apart the two halves of a perforated card and handed one half to Matt. "If you'll give this to the front desk when you check in, we'll have your bags delivered to your room momentarily."

"Thank you," Matt said and came around to my side to take my hand.

"I feel underdressed," I whispered, zipping up my

windbreaker. My jeans and light sweater weren't ratty by any means, but they didn't feel as high society as this place looked.

"You're fine." Matt kissed my cheek and led me up the stairs to the entrance, where a bellman opened the door for us.

I gasped before my foot even hit the marble floor. The foyer or lobby or whatever you'd call it in a house-turned-hotel like that was massive. The ceilings were at least two stories high, and massive columns supported archways that separated different areas of the space. For a second, I felt like a turn-of-the-century socialite arriving for a party.

"Welcome to the Alford Inn. Are you checking in?"

I turned slowly to the girl at the desk, my eyes still trying to take everything in. The sight of the desk broke the spell. The conversion to a hotel hadn't been able to preserve all of the house's grandeur after all.

I followed Matt over to the desk where a pretty girl in her early twenties stood with a bright smile on her face. "Your name, please?"

"Matt Cardosi."

"Do you have a luggage ticket?"

I gazed around the room some more as they handled all the boring details of the checking-in process. Now that I wasn't feeling so much like I'd walked into a fairy tale, I noticed the places where the building's opulence had made concessions to the business needs of a hotel. While they'd kept the glamour of the entrance with period chairs and décor, I could see where they'd made a lounge area with comfy-looking contemporary furnishings in the back. And the elevator off to the side was decidedly modern looking. But I didn't care, because the place was gorgeous whether parts of it were modernized or not.

"So I have you down for a couples massage on Sunday morning. Is that right?"

"You planned for us to have a couples massage?" I cut in before Matt could answer.

He smiled a smile that made my insides feel all mushy. "I have lots of things planned for you this weekend. Just wait and see." He slipped his arm around my waist and pulled me close, putting his lips to mine in a kiss that probably wasn't quite appropriate for the setting.

I giggled and pulled away. "Stop it!" I blushed and glanced at the girl at the desk. She must have been well trained because her expression was totally neutral and her eyes were glued to the computer screen in front of her.

"Yes, a couples massage on Sunday morning," Matt said.

She smiled and nodded, clicking a few things on the computer. "Do you want me to review the rest of your bookings with you now, or should we keep those a secret a little longer?"

"Can I come back down later and go over it?" I asked.

"You sure can."

"Actually, do you have a pamphlet or anything that lists all your amenities?"

"Of course! Let me just grab one for you." She bent down behind the desk. "I know they're down here somewhere. There will also be a book in your room listing all our offerings. It's nice because it has bigger pictures and longer descriptions, but the brochure is good to have handy too. Oh, there they are! It looks like we have just a couple left, but I'm sure we have more in the back."

Before she could stand back up, a door in the back burst open. "Whitney! What are you doing down there? There are guests at the desk."

"Yes, I was just getting—"

"Have they even been greeted properly?" He turned to us with a cloying smile and a suddenly smooth tone that was a world away from the way he'd snapped at Whitney. "Welcome to the Alford Inn. My name is Garrett, and I'm the manager here. I'm terribly sorry for my employee's rudeness."

"Oh, no, she's—" I started to defend her, but Garrett cut me off.

"What name are you checking in under, please, sir?"

"Whitney already started checking us in," Matt said, his voice low and his jaw tight.

"Excellent then. You can see why I'd be confused when I saw you standing there while she crawled around on the floor."

Whitney, who had stood back up right after he appeared out of nowhere and started barking at her, flushed a dark red that was visible even on her caramel-colored skin.

"She was looking for a brochure about your amenities for me," I said, trying to make the situation better.

For some reason, that seemed to make him more upset. He glared at Whitney. "You didn't tell her there's a book in the room? No one knows how to do their job around here!"

At the rate she was blinking, I knew she was about to break down.

"Yes, she told me about the book, but I asked for a brochure, so she was getting me a brochure," I snapped.

"Well!" He straightened his vest and glanced around like he was looking for something else to criticize. "If she had just told me that up front, we wouldn't have had this little incident, would we?"

I took a breath and opened my mouth, but Matt saw it coming and stopped me. "Now that that's all worked out, how about we finish checking in." He looked at Whitney—who was still fighting back tears—and smiled. "Whitney?"

Garrett stood back and gestured at the computer

like she was somehow deficient for not teleporting the two-foot distance in the half second that had gone by since Matt spoke.

She stepped forward and took her place back at the computer. She scrolled her mouse and clicked a few times. "So, like I said, you have a couples massage scheduled for Sunday morning—" Her voice was almost whisper quiet now and had none of the enthusiasm it had contained just minutes earlier.

"Speak up so they can hear you!" Garrett spat as he hovered just over her shoulder.

I gave him the smile I reserve for my very most difficult customers at the café—the ones who ordered a macchiato and complained that it didn't have enough milk in it then argued with me when I suggested that perhaps they'd prefer a cappuccino or latte instead of a drink that, by definition, had just a little bit of milk in it. "She's actually fine. We both have excellent hearing, and I have a bit of a headache right now that makes loud noises rather painful." I was lying, but I would do whatever it took to get him to leave her alone.

His mouth twitched, like it was resisting what he was trying to get it to do. Finally, he managed to say, "Good job, then, Whitney," before turning on his heel and disappearing back through the door he'd come from.

As soon as the door clicked closed, I saw Whitney's chin tremble for a second before she bit her lip and held it still. "Thank you," she said quietly.

"Is he always like that?" My voice was at a near whisper because, just from what I'd seen, I wouldn't have put it past him to be listening at the door.

Her shoulder twitched. "Sometimes. Sometimes he's really nice though."

Now I bit my lip to keep myself from going off on a tirade about what I thought of him and the situation and what she should do about it. It wasn't the time or place.

Matt, apparently sensing my discomfort, put a comforting hand on my lower back, and I leaned into him.

"Okay, you guys are all checked in." Whitney picked up a little envelope and handed it to Matt. "Your key cards are inside. You'll be in room 345. That'll be on the left-hand side of the hotel, in the new portion, toward the back. You can get there by taking either of the lobby elevators or by going down the hall, turning right past the bakery and gift shop, and taking the elevator at the end of that hallway. Would you like a bellman to show you the way?"

"I think we can find it," Matt said, smiling. "Thank you for all your help. You were very gracious."

She smiled sadly and batted her eyes, fighting back more tears. "Thank you. Whenever you want to come down and review your bookings, you can. Enjoy your stay."

"Thanks, we will." Matt and I stepped away from the desk. "So which elevator do you want to take?"

I shrugged. I wanted to explore the whole hotel at some point but didn't see the point in traipsing off to find a different elevator when there was one right in front of me. "This one's fine."

We got on the elevator, and Matt pushed the button for the third floor. Just as the door started to close, I heard a man's voice talking to someone as he approached down the hallway.

"I was thinking we'd have dinner at one of the hotel restaurants tonight. What do you think?" The voice sounded strangely familiar, but the door closed before I could get a look at who it was.

I blinked a couple of times and looked at Matt. "Was that… Mike?"

Matt looked at me like I'd lost my mind. "I don't think so. Why would he even be here?"

I couldn't think of a single reason why he would.

Chapter 3

OUR ROOM WAS in the newer part of the hotel that lacked the Gilded Age glamour of the old part but still was probably the nicest hotel I'd ever been in. And while our room was pretty much the farthest it could possibly be from the front desk, there was a reason for that. It was on one of the back corners of the U-shaped hotel and had windows on two sides that looked out on a breathtaking view of the mountains. And, based on the plaque outside the door, it was one of the rooms celebrities stayed in when they came. That's the kind of hotel it was—the kind that movie stars vacationed at.

Matt flopped down on the couch and turned on the TV while I wandered around the room—it was big enough to wander around—and looked at everything. The bed had fluffy pillows covered with silky pillowcases. I reached under the duvet to check, and the sheets were just as silky.

In the bathroom, the high-end toiletries nearly distracted me from how soft and fluffy the towels were. And the fact that there was a massive free-standing bathtub with bath bombs and little packages of bubble bath around it. And the fully tiled shower with a rain head. I wasn't going to be fooled by that though. I'd stayed in enough hotels where the water pressure was barely enough to wash my hands, let alone my thick mop of hair. I turned the shower on, just to see. It had actual water pressure. Enough to wash my hair in less than half an hour.

I was officially in love with this hotel.

"What are you doing in there? Are you taking a shower?" Matt called from the other room.

"Nope, just checking the water pressure," I said, walking back out and crossing the sitting area to go toward what looked like a balcony on the far side of the room.

Matt gave me a look like I was crazy.

"If you had thick hair, you'd understand."

He still looked at me like I'd lost a few marbles. I ignored him and pushed open the sheer curtains covering a set of French doors. I opened the doors and stepped onto the balcony. Somehow the view was even more breathtaking from out there. I could see for miles. I walked over to the thick stone railing and looked down the side of the hotel. As far as I could tell, our room and the ones above and below it had balconies.

I walked over to the other side of the balcony. From there, I could see across to the other side of the hotel's U and down to the courtyard at its bottom. A massive balcony off the hotel lobby spanned the space just beyond the courtyard. It had scattered chairs for guests to lounge in and watch the sunset and a section of tables that I guessed belonged to one of the hotel's restaurants. Between me and the courtyard was the entrance to the underground spa. As gorgeous as the room was, I really wanted to go explore the hotel and see that spa.

"Let's go explore!" I said, popping back into the room.

Matt didn't budge. "Hold on." He pointed at the TV with the remote. "Look at this. They have a whole channel about the golf course."

"I want to go see the spa."

"There's one about the spa too." He changed the channel, and the cave-like entrance to the spa popped up on the screen.

"But we could see it in person."

"They have one that's just about the restaurants too."

"I'm going to go explore the hotel."

As I expected, Matt popped up. "Okay, I'm coming."

We took the elevator closest to our room down to

the first floor and started to wander back toward the lobby. The gift shop was across from the bakery. The French bakery. With the famous French pastry chef. And *Pâtisserie Alford* in big gold letters across the transom above the door and front window, with *Jacques de Gaulle, Chef* in slightly smaller gold letters underneath it. It looked just like a real French patisserie, like you'd find on a romantic vacation in Paris. Or any other trip to Paris, but I had romance on my mind. I couldn't help but stare in awe.

"Do you want me to take a picture of you in front of it?"

I looked at Matt, suddenly breaking out of my fantasy of being on a Parisian street corner. "What? No!" I said emphatically as my brain tried to get me to say the opposite.

The corner of Matt's mouth twitched up knowingly. "Go on, stand by the door." He was already reaching into his pocket to pull out his phone.

"Matty, no, I—"

"You know you want to," he teased.

Yes, I did, but—"I don't want the people who work in there to think I'm crazy."

"There's no one in there. Just do it real quick, and I'll get a picture."

He was right. There was no one at the counter. But that didn't mean they weren't inside somewhere watching. Still, it was Jacques de Gaulle's bakery. "Okay, just be quick about it." I dashed over to the front of the bakery and posed while Matt snapped a few pictures then went back over to him to look at them.

"Happy?" he asked as he scrolled through them.

I was. They were actually good pictures of me, and he'd gotten the name of the bakery in the shot.

"Want to go in?"

"I want to look at the window first." It was beautiful. Down one side was a full rainbow spectrum of perfectly executed macarons, then the rest of the case was filled up with beautiful mille-feuille, chocolate and fruit tarts, eclairs, cakes, and more.

"Looks fancy," Matt said beside me.

"Looks delicious," I countered.

"Ready to go in?"

I could have stood there and stared at the window all day long, but I wasn't going to be able to eat any of it if I didn't go in. Besides, there were more delicious-looking pastries inside for me to drool over.

If I expected someone to greet us when we walked in, I was going to be disappointed. No one came out from the back when we walked in. I took the opportunity to peruse the display case. There were so many things I wanted to try. I'd had most of them before but never ones made by Jacques de Gaulle.

"Is there a bell or something?" Matt leaned over the counter. He was obviously not as interested in examining the display case as I was.

"Maybe they're in the back." I moved over to the

macaron case. They were on their own, separate from everything else. Like the window, they were arranged by color, in rainbow order. I mentally debated between picking out the ones that looked most delicious and starting out by trying those or just starting at the top left corner and working my way through them in order.

"Hello?" Matt angled his head to try to see through the window in the door to the back.

I decided to pick out the macarons I wanted most. I would never be able to work myself through all of them, and I'd probably get sick from all the sugar before I even got to the yellow lemon-flavored ones that looked so good.

"Anybody back there?"

Matt would probably want to try a chocolate one. I, of course, wanted to try the coffee-flavored ones but was also intrigued by the lavender-coconut ones. I wasn't sure that I would like them, but if they were made by a world-renowned pastry chef, they couldn't be that bad.

Matt walked over to stand beside me. "I don't think anyone's here."

"Someone must be here. It's open, isn't it?"

"They must not want to sell us anything then because they're not coming out."

"I'm sure they'll be out in a minute." I had to admit, the strawberry cheesecake ones looked good too.

Matt peeked over my shoulder. "What are those? Some kind of sandwich cookies?"

"They're macarons. They're amazing. They're delicate and chewy but crunchy and—"

"Macarons? You mean macaroons?"

"No, macaroons are the coconut ones. These are mac*arons*. They're French."

"They're really good or something?"

"They're outstanding. The shell—that's the cookie part—has a little bit of a crunch, and then it's soft and chewy in the middle. And then you have the filling. That's usually something creamy, but you can see those have a kind of jam in the middle."

Matt nodded. "And they come in different flavors?"

"Yup. See, they have raspberry and rose"—Matt made a face, but I kept going— "and chocolate and lime. Pretty much any flavor you can imagine."

"Sounds good. I'd try one." He looked around the bakery again. "Too bad there's no one here to sell us one."

I had to admit, it was getting a little ridiculous. Someone definitely should have shown up by now. Even if they were working in the back, they should have at least checked for customers.

"How about we go over to the gift shop and look around for a while? Maybe someone will show up by then."

I was reluctant to leave the wonderland of

pastries, but it didn't do me any good to stand there and stare if there was no one to get anything out for me.

I agreed, and we walked across the hall to the gift shop, which was full of souvenirs from the hotel and the Berkshires in general, as well as products made in the area. Among the baskets and wall hangings and hand-sketched postcards of the hotel, I found a macaron cookbook written by Jacques de Gaulle. It was the only one they had out, and while I knew they might have more in the back, I didn't want to give anyone else the chance to snap it up if they didn't.

"You planning to start making macarons?" Matt asked.

I shrugged. "Maybe."

"For the café?"

This time, I shook my head rapidly. "Nooo," I said, drawing out the word.

Matt's eyebrows rose.

I shook my head again. "They're too finicky. I mean, they're not *hard*, and they're still delicious even if they go a little wrong, but to get them right every single time—and they have to be right to sell them— things have to be more controlled than they are in the café. I'd probably start making the meringue and get distracted by a customer and end up with it completely over whipped. And then if it was too humid one day, the shells might not dry out right or—"

Matt stared at me, obviously having no idea what I was talking about.

"Never mind. There are a lot of variables that affect the end result, and I'd rather just leave it to the professionals."

"You're a professional."

"I mean the professional bakers."

"You're a professional baker. You bake for the café every day."

"You know what I mean."

Matt smiled at me with a soft look in his eyes. "I do, but I don't like seeing you sell yourself short. You can do anything you set your mind to. Even solving crimes. I know. I've seen you do it." He pulled me into his arms and kissed me on the top of my head then on my temple then my cheek then my lips—

I pulled away, smiling at him. "We should finish looking around."

"Hmm, if you say so." His eyes twinkled mischievously. "Or we could duck behind those clothing racks over there."

I laughed and swatted at him with my cookbook. "Let's not. We just got here, and I don't want to get kicked out."

Matt chuckled, but let it drop.

When we finished looking around, we made our way up to the register.

The woman behind the counter smiled and

greeted us. "Oh, you got very lucky," she said when she saw the book. "You snagged our last copy!"

"Oh really?" I was glad I'd decided to go ahead and get it instead of waiting until the end of the visit.

She nodded. "It was a very limited printing." She leaned toward us with a conspiratorial smile. "I don't think Jacques wanted too many people getting his secrets!"

"Then why did he publish a book at all?"

Her eyes lit up. "For the publicity! For the mystique! According to him, having a rare cookbook is better than having no cookbook at all, even if it means that some of his secrets get out."

I knew from experience that a good recipe only went so far. You had to know how to execute it too. Especially with something as complex as macarons. "I doubt anyone could replicate his macarons even if they had the recipes."

"You're right about that." She pulled out a piece of tissue paper and started wrapping the book up. "Are you two just arriving or just leaving?"

"We just got here."

She patted the tissue-wrapped book. "You should get him to sign this before you go. He's almost always in the back there. Works too much, if you ask me, but he doesn't. Just ask Sophie to call him out for you."

I glanced over at the bakery. The counter was still empty. "Are they closed right now? The door was open, but there was no one in there when we went a few minutes ago, and there's still no one there."

The woman craned her neck to look then huffed impatiently. "That girl!" She shook her head. "She's always wandering off like she has better things to do than *her job*. I'll mention it to Jacques." She sighed again. "But no, they're not closed. I'd tell you to just poke your head in the back, but he gets touchy about guests being in his space. Just check back. She'll show up sooner or later." She held up the bag she'd slipped the book into. "Are you headed back to your room, or would you like me to send this up for you so you don't have to carry it around?"

I glanced at Matt, who shrugged. "Send it up, I guess." The bellmen still had to deliver our luggage at some point anyway.

We thanked her and headed out. I couldn't wait to see the spa.

Chapter 4

WE MADE our way toward the lobby, where there was an exit to the courtyard. And, of course, in the courtyard was the entrance to the spa.

Matt, however, lacking my single-minded focus on exploration, got distracted by the lounge off the back of the lobby. "Found the bar," he said as he veered off.

I didn't follow him, figuring that if I did, I would just be contributing to my mission being derailed. "I thought we were going to the spa."

"We are. I just want to check things out back here."

I crossed my arms and stayed put.

"Aw, come on, Franny. The spa isn't going to pick up and leave. It'll still be there when we get there."

I sighed. I really wanted to get down there. I wanted to see what it looked like and what services they offered and if they had any openings, maybe even later that day. But Matt was looking at me imploringly, and it wouldn't really hurt anything to just go take a look at the lounge. I sighed and followed him across the lobby and into the lounge.

After seeing the rest of the hotel, I shouldn't have been surprised that it was an impressive space, but I was. Large and spacious with comfortable-looking furniture scattered all around, it was like a really upscale living room but on steroids. A grand piano sat in one corner near an open area and a parquet floor, which I guessed were used for bands and dancing. I suddenly knew where I wanted to spend the evening.

And that was before I really focused on the other side of the room, which was dominated by a large, well-stocked bar and, beside that, a smaller but still well-stocked coffee bar. Both of which were currently unattended although neither had any kind of sign saying that they were closed or when they'd reopen.

"Does *anyone* work here?" I asked to myself and the empty room as much as to Matt.

"Probably doesn't open until the evening," Matt said, picking up a menu book from the bar counter. "They have desserts too."

"What about the coffee bar though? I like an after-dinner coffee as much as anyone, but it's not exactly peak coffee time."

Matt shrugged. If it wasn't Boston sports, he didn't get worked up about it. "Maybe just on a break, then."

He wandered over to the windows that covered the entire back wall, giving access to the balcony for one thing and a stunning view of the mountains for another.

"They should really have a sign or something."

I looked over their offerings. They had a good variety, with beans from Hawaii, Ethiopia, and Costa Rica. I even spotted a bag of my personal favorite coffee beans that I usually only allowed myself to splurge on once a year or so. I found myself really annoyed that whoever was supposed to be manning the bar was missing. I would have really liked to indulge in a cup right then and drink it while I sat out on the balcony, gazing at the landscape. I would have even been willing to postpone my visit to the spa for it.

Matt walked up behind me and slipped his arms around my waist. He brushed a kiss against my neck. "Don't worry, Franny. I'm sure he'll be back. How about we go down and take a look at the spa now? We can stop by here again on our way to the room."

I sighed and turned to head to the spa. It was the lack of customer service that bothered me more than anything. Here I was, a paying customer who just wanted some macarons and a cup of coffee—maybe a macchiato so I could really taste those beans I liked —and I couldn't find a single person to help me. Maybe I should go mention the missing barista to the lady in the gift shop too since she'd seemed interested in the fact that the girl at the patisserie was missing.

Just as we were walking past the bar, a handsome twentysomething came through the door behind the bar. Based on his black shirt and pants and the black striped apron he was tying on, I assumed he was the bartender finally showing up for work.

"Hey, guys, how's it going?" He grinned, baring sparkling white teeth that, with his ocean-blue eyes and movie-star hair, made me think that he probably did pretty well in the tip department. And that a hotel was a dangerous place for him to work.

Matt, of course, wasn't fazed in the least by the fact that this guy had only just now shown up after we'd been wandering around for five minutes. "We're good. Just heading down to check out the spa. How about you?"

"I'm good!" He grinned again. This time I noticed that he looked slightly out of breath. He was breathing hard but trying to cover it. Probably because he didn't want to make it any more painfully obvious than it already was that he was late to his post. "The spa's great. You'll love it!" He pointed at me and smiled the smile of a man who was used to women falling at his feet. It didn't work on me, but I did have to admit that it was rather charming.

I wasn't going to let on about that though. I was still annoyed that both bars had been unattended when we got there. "I wanted a cup of coffee before I went down there, but nobody was here."

The bartender looked over at the coffee bar,

apparently surprised to see that it was empty. "I'm sorry about that, miss. Carrick has a tendency to wander off sometimes. Thinks he's too good for his job or something." He chuckled, but I wasn't sure whether it was actually because he was joking or because he wasn't. "I can make you a cup if you want though. I may not know how to make all the fancy peppermint caramel soy mochaccino things, but I can try." He smiled again, and I felt my resistance to him melting. At least he was friendly when he was at the bar instead of seeming annoyed by it.

Matt pulled me toward him with his arm around my waist and kissed my hair. "Franny actually owns a coffee shop, so she knows how to make all those things."

"Oh yeah?" The bartender's eyes lit up, and he smiled again. "I'm not supposed to let you behind the counter, but if you can walk me through it, I'll make you whatever you want. On the house too. As an apology for no one being here."

I mentally debated whether to have him make me something or just to go down to the spa, like I'd planned. On the one hand, I couldn't wait to get down to the spa. On the other... well, coffee. "Do you know if there are any of those Ecuadorian beans roasted?"

He walked over to the coffee bar and inspected the shelves above and below the counter before popping up with a small container of coffee grounds. "Is this the one?"

I'd been hoping for fresh-ground, but since he'd gone to the trouble of looking for me, I went with it. "That's it!"

"A'right, what do you want?"

I walked him through the steps to make me a macchiato. It was not the most complex drink, so he mostly had it under control, but I did give him a tip or two here and there to get the best result. He was actually a good student and looked at me expectantly as he handed over the cup.

I sipped it cautiously and smiled. "It's good!"

He pumped his fist and let out a satisfied, "Yes!"

"I would actually be happy to have this served in my café."

"That's high praise coming from her," Matt said. "She is pi-*cky*." He drew the word out in emphasis.

"Hey!" I swatted at him but happily went back for another sip. The bartender really had done a good job. Maybe all the drink-making skills were stored in the same place in his brain, so his experience bartending paid off in his coffee-making. But whatever the reason, he made a good cup. All my irritation melted away as I swallowed down the steamy liquid. Some people, coffee woke up. Me, it relaxed.

I finished my cup and thanked the bartender.

"No problem. And sorry again that nobody was out here. I'll talk to Carrick about it when he shows back up. Oh, I'm Tommy, by the way." He reached his hand out to shake both of ours.

We shook and introduced ourselves.

"Just ask for me if you need anything. And enjoy the spa! It's really nice down there. You guys will like it."

I thanked him, and we headed out to the lobby to resume our mission.

Whitney hurried past us on her way back to the desk from… somewhere. Was anyone in this place ever where they should be? It wasn't my problem. I wasn't going to let it bother me—much. Besides, there were lots of reasons for people to be off somewhere other than the counter they were supposed to stand behind. Maybe Whitney had been helping a guest. And maybe Tommy had been on break. Lots of reasons.

When Whitney caught sight of us, she smiled and slowed her brisk walk. "You guys find your room okay?"

"Sure did," Matt said cheerfully.

"Great! If there's anything else you need, just let me know."

"Will do."

Whitney hurried away, and I looked around for the door to the spa. I knew I'd seen it earlier, when we were checking in. As my eyes swept the room, they glanced across the closing elevator door. I did a double take. "Was that Sandra?"

"Sandra?" Matt looked confused.

"Sandra Stanton. Mike's wife."

Now he looked tired. He put his hands on my shoulders and looked me in the eyes. "First you think you see Mike, and now you think you see Sandra? Come on, Franny. You've got to get your mind off Cape Bay. Disconnect. That's what we're here for, remember?" His eyes searched mine, presumably hoping to find some shred of calm hiding somewhere in them.

I smiled and nodded. "Right. No more thinking about Cape Bay or anyone in it. Just rest and relaxation."

He smiled in relief. "Good."

"You know where I've heard is a good place to relax?"

"Where?" he asked good-naturedly even though I was pretty sure he already knew what I was going to say.

"In the spa!"

He chuckled. "Yeah, I guess if we'd gone straight there, you wouldn't have had a chance to start thinking about Cape Bay again."

"You're right." I grinned. "It's your fault."

"Well, let me make it up to you, then." He took my hand in his, and we finally—finally!—headed straight for the spa.

The cave-like entrance was inside what looked from one angle like a pile of rocks just beyond the courtyard. Walking through the doors, I already felt like I was a world away.

The spa's lobby was down a long, rock-lined hallway. The woman at the counter smiled warmly when she saw us approach.

"Welcome to the Spa at the Alford Inn. Do you have a treatment scheduled?" Her voice was soft and low—exactly the kind of voice people wanted in a spa.

"We have a couples massage Sunday," Matt said a little too loudly in the quiet space. "She just wanted to take a look around today."

"Excellent. Let me just call Noelle up to give you a tour." She picked up a phone next to her and spoke even more softly into it, so softly that I wondered how the person on the other end could even hear her. She put the phone down and turned her warm smile on me. "Perhaps you'd like to see our list of services?" She pulled a thick brochure from a stack and passed it to me.

I had just begun to look through it when a woman came up beside us. "Hi, I'm Noelle. Are you ready for your tour?"

We followed Noelle through a set of double doors and into the spa itself. She showed us the locker rooms —by far the nicest locker rooms I'd ever seen, more like a department store dressing room than anything else—the mineral water swimming pool in a space designed to make you feel like you were in a forgotten grotto, and a room she called the mixed-gender quiet room.

"There are, of course, single-gender quiet rooms off each locker room, but this space is for everyone," she said so softly I had to lean in to hear. "On that wall, you'll find a variety of herbal teas and flavored waters for you to enjoy while you repose. Down this hall are our treatment rooms." She gestured to a dim hallway lined with doors. A woman in all white opened one of the doors and stepped inside. "Soft conversation is allowed, but we do ask that you be cognizant of other guests who may prefer a quieter rest."

A bloodcurdling scream broke the silence.

Our tour guide looked startled as she turned her head back and forth, looking for who had shattered the near silence. Everyone looked just as startled as she was though.

Another scream. And another. Then a door down the hallway burst open, and the woman I'd just seen enter flung herself out.

"Oh my God!" she screamed. "She's dead!"

Chapter 5

CHAOS ERUPTED as all the people who had been relaxing in the quiet room only seconds before started screaming and running for the exit. Several of the treatment room doors opened. Spa employees, dressed in white, peeked out. Some of them had guests in white robes push out past them and head for the exit. So much for relaxation.

"Everyone, please stay calm." Noelle's voice had come up to what seemed like normal conversation volume as she tried in vain to keep people from knocking over tables and chairs and carafes of cucumber water in their mad dash for the doors. More quietly, she said into a microphone attached to an earpiece I had only just noticed, "Front desk, we have a code black. Request security to the treatment rooms and call 911." She turned and smiled serenely at us, an expression that seemed wildly out of place.

"I'm so sorry, but we'll have to cut our tour short. If you'll leave your names and room number with the front desk, we'll contact you as soon as we have things under control and are ready to resume business as usual." The calm smile stayed plastered on her face.

For a moment, I thought she had lost her mind. Or maybe she'd never had it in the first place. Maybe she'd lost it a long time ago, after too many days spent whispering to strangers about peaceful grottos and quiet repose. But as soon as Matt made the slightest motion toward the exit, she turned and ran down the treatment hallway. I grabbed Matt's arm to stop him. Something about the way the girl had screamed made me want to stay and see what was going on.

"Amber! What's going on? Who's dead?" Noelle's voice was suddenly much louder and thick with a Boston accent that had been undetectable in her controlled spa technician voice.

Amber, the girl who had burst out of the room screaming, pointed back into it with one hand while she covered her mouth with the other.

Noelle looked inside. "Who is it? A guest?"

Amber shook her head. "Gina!"

"Gina? She's not on the schedule for today. What was she doing here?"

Amber sank down to the floor. "She wanted me to give her a treatment."

Noelle walked slowly toward the door to the room. "But what—what happened?"

"I don't know!" Amber gasped. "I was giving her a mud wrap, and I got her all wrapped up and left to let it dry, like I always do, and when I came back, her face was covered! I thought maybe she did it, so I pulled the strip off—"

"How would she do it?" Noelle interrupted. "Her arms are wrapped up against her!"

"I don't know!" Amber's voice came out as a shriek. "I didn't think about it! I just pulled the strip off, and her lips were blue, and she was dead!"

"Come on. Let's get out of here," Matt said quietly and pulled at my arm.

I waved my hand at him.

Noelle pulled the microphone up to her mouth again. "Tell 911 we need the police too. I think Gina's been murdered."

Matt pulled my arm again, and this time I let him. I felt nauseous as I stumbled after him. A murder? Here? At the spa? At the gorgeous historic hotel? Didn't I get enough of those back in Cape Bay?

I followed him blindly through the halls back up to the lobby. I was glad he was leading me because I wasn't sure that I could have found the way on my own. Not with my mind reeling like it was.

We got close to the lobby but couldn't get in because it was packed full of the people who'd been enjoying their time at the spa until moments before. Hotel security was blocking the doors and only letting people out one by one as they took down their names and room numbers. The spa workers were milling around, alternately making weak efforts to calm down anxious spa-goers and hugging each other with tears pouring down their faces. Obviously, they'd already heard that the dead person was someone they knew.

Since I'd made us wait to hear what had happened, Matt and I were at the back of the group of people trying to get out of the spa and had to wait what felt like an eternity to be allowed to leave. We were both in shock and didn't have much to say while we waited, but Matt held tight to my hand like he was afraid to let me go.

At some point, the police arrived. They must have come in through a back door because they just popped through a door behind me, and I didn't even see them until they were halfway down the hall toward the treatment rooms. There was a whole troop of them, which I guessed made sense for a murder investigation—three or four officers in uniforms and another three in plain clothes.

For a second, I was sure that one of the plain-clothes officers was Mike, my friend and local detective from back home—the same Mike I thought I'd heard and whose wife I thought I'd seen. But I told myself I was being ridiculous. I was just used to seeing Mike at crime scenes. There was no reason for him to be here in the hotel. I didn't even say anything about it to Matt, knowing that he'd tell me I was thinking too much about Cape Bay. And I was.

Having all that time to stand still and do nothing while we waited to be let out had given my mind a chance to wander, and it wandered straight to Cape Bay. Even though I knew I'd left the café in good hands with Sammy, I worried about it. Worried that she wouldn't have enough help, worried that she'd miss something in the supply order, worried that there would be some kind of disaster and the whole place would be flooded when I got back. Logically, I knew that everything would almost definitely be fine and there was almost definitely nothing to worry about, but that didn't stop my mind from racing.

I missed my dog too. What I wouldn't give for a good snuggle with Latte about now.

When we were finally allowed out of the spa (after agreeing not to leave the hotel without notifying the front desk and giving them a number where we could be reached), all I wanted to do was go back up to our room and forget about what had happened in the spa.

But when we got to the lobby, Matt veered off suddenly. "I need a drink."

I needed a long, hot bath filled with good-smelling fizzy things, but he still had a firm hold on my hand, so I didn't have much choice but to follow along. Of course, a drink didn't sound too bad either.

The lounge actually had people milling around it now, many of them in the white robes they'd left the spa in. I was glad I was dressed.

Matt walked us over to the bar where Tommy was

looking harried. His eyes were red, and he looked more disheveled than he had an hour ago. "Hey, guys, what can I get for you?" he asked, not making eye contact as he wiped the bar with a cloth.

"Scotch. Straight," Matt said.

I looked at him in surprise. I didn't think I'd ever seen him drink scotch, especially not straight. But I realized that, while I'd had the misfortune of being around a couple of dead bodies, this was his first. Even when his dad died, I was the one who found him, not Matt.

"Scotch, straight," Tommy repeated. He looked at me. "And you?"

"Ummm…" I tried to glance covertly at the still-unattended coffee bar, but I must not have been very successful.

"I got you," Tommy said, giving me a weak smile.

I realized then that he didn't look disheveled from the sudden rush of customers but because he'd heard that there had been a death. And possibly that it was one of his coworkers. And maybe even that they suspected murder. I wondered if he'd known Gina.

He poured Matt's scotch and passed it across the bar. Matt tossed it back without flinching, and I wondered if this was a new skill or if he'd always been able to down liquor like that.

He gave me a sideways smile. "My friends liked to go out drinking back in college."

His *friends*. Sure.

"You want another one?" Tommy asked Matt.

"A beer. Whatever you have on tap."

Tommy poured Matt's beer and passed it over then looked at me and tilted his head in the direction of the coffee bar. I followed him over. "Same thing?" he asked.

I shook my head. "Just an espresso."

"That's it? You want anything in it?" He gestured toward the bar.

"No thanks."

"Really?" He looked skeptical, proving that he was a bartender, not a barista, at heart. "Not even some Irish cream?"

I thought about that for a second and then nodded. It couldn't hurt. It might even taste good.

He grabbed the Irish cream from the bar while the espresso was brewing then poured it in and handed it over to me.

I took a sip and nodded. He nodded with something that looked like an attempt at a smile on his face. I turned to walk back over to Matt but then realized that Tommy was still standing at the counter, watching me. I raised my eyebrows. He leaned in.

"So, you were, uh, were you down there when they—when they found…?" His voice trailed off.

I nodded.

"Who—who was it?" His voice was tight, like he had to work to push it out of his throat.

"They said her name was Gina."

His knees buckled, but he caught himself with his hands braced against the counter. I waited for him to regain his composure.

"You knew her?" I asked.

He nodded. "She's a friend. We grew up together."

"I'm sorry."

He nodded again. "Thank you for telling me." His voice had gone from tight to hoarse. He glanced over at the bar, where a white-robed man was impatiently drumming his fingers. "Better get back to work."

I watched as he dealt calmly with the irritated customer and felt bad for him. He'd just found out that a friend of his was dead, and he still had to deal with people who were annoyed that they were inconvenienced by their spa visit ending early. It didn't seem fair.

I walked back over to Matt and drank my spiked espresso while he finished his beer.

"You ready to go upstairs?" he asked after he left some bills for Tommy.

"More than ready." Nothing sounded better than to go to the room and sink down into a hot bath. Then maybe take a nap or sit on the balcony and admire the scenery. Or maybe both. Whatever it took to get my mind off the dead girl in the spa and her friend's sad face.

Chapter 6

I COULDN'T SETTLE DOWN. I couldn't relax. I tried sitting on the balcony, but I was too restless. I tried watching TV, but I couldn't focus. I tried taking a nap, but every time I closed my eyes, I saw the look on Amber's face in the spa as she stumbled out of the treatment room. Matt didn't have that problem apparently. He flopped down on the bed as soon as we walked in the door, turned the TV to ESPN, and passed out cold.

I wandered into the bathroom. Maybe a bath in that giant, luxurious bathtub would do the trick. But as I stood there looking at it, I knew I wouldn't appreciate it. I would use up those high-end products and probably spend five minutes in it before I got too fidgety and had to get out.

I wandered back into the bedroom and looked at Matt snoring away on the big soft bed with its fluffy pillows and blankets. He looked so peaceful lying there. Peaceful was the last thing I was.

I went over to the desk and pulled out one of the sheets of writing paper they had in the drawer. I ran my fingers across the cross-hatched surface of the paper. Even the stationery in this place was high-end. I grabbed one of the pens—just a basic ballpoint— and scribbled out a note to Matt then double-checked that I had my key and slipped out the door.

As I passed the bakery, I was happy to see that someone was actually working at the counter now. There were several people waiting, one of them still inexplicably in a white robe even though they must have had a good hour by then to change, so I kept walking. At least I knew now that someone did work there occasionally and there was a chance I could catch her again before I left.

The crowd that had evacuated the spa had mostly cleared out of the lounge by the time I wandered back in. There were a few people scattered around the spacious room, all of whom were, thankfully, wearing real clothes. I headed for the bar. The coffee bar was somehow still unattended, but I knew that Tommy would take care of me no matter what I wanted.

Halfway across the room, I stopped in my tracks. I'd let my gaze drift over to the wall of windows and out to the mountains. That wasn't what startled me though. What startled me was the man sitting in one of the chairs out on the balcony. All I could see was the back of his head, but it looked just like the back of Mike Stanton's head. Why I thought that from just a glimpse of a high and tight haircut, I don't know, but for a second, I was sure it was Mike. And then I told myself that I was being ridiculous. Lots of men had that hairstyle. Whatever was making me keep thinking I saw Mike or his wife, I needed to let it go.

I walked over to the bar and slid onto a barstool. Tommy walked up and put a coaster and a cocktail napkin down in front of me. "Back again already?"

"Yup," I sighed.

"Forgot your man this time."

I laughed softly. Something about him calling Matt my "man" struck me as funny. "He's taking a nap in our room."

"But you're not?"

I shook my head. "No. I just kept thinking about —" I waved my hand in the general direction of the courtyard and the spa entrance.

"Yeah, me too," he said, his voice soft and a little raspy. He looked away at something at the far end of the bar.

"She was a friend?" I asked quietly.

He nodded, still looking away.

"I'm sorry."

"Thanks," he said and wiped absently at the bar with a cloth. He took a deep breath and finally looked back at me with glassy eyes. "What can I get you?"

I ignored the question. "Can you go take a break?

Have you even had a minute to yourself since you found out?"

He shook his head and gestured toward the empty coffee bar. "No one to cover for me."

I wished I could tell him to just go sit down in the back for a minute, but I wasn't his boss. "Where is he anyway? Did he just not show up for his shift?"

Tommy shrugged. "He's here somewhere. I saw him earlier. Might be down in the spa or something."

"That doesn't seem fair."

"Carrick doesn't care much about fair."

"And he gets away with it?"

"So far." He nodded at someone behind me, another customer getting ready to leave, I guessed. He took another deep breath and gave me something like a smile. "Now I know you didn't come down here to talk about all that. What can I get for you?"

I stared at the menu and racked my brain. I didn't want anything too strong, but I didn't want to just ask for a glass of water either.

"Need some help?"

I nodded. I could pick out a coffee drink any day of the week for any time or occasion, but cocktails weren't my strong suit.

He narrowed his eyes and tilted his head, studying my face for a minute. "You look like a…"

For a second, I was afraid he was going to blurt out some unexpected insult about having dark circles under my eyes. Thank goodness, he didn't.

"…rosé spritzer kind of girl."

I wasn't—club soda wasn't my thing—but I agreed anyway. And I was glad that I did. The drink he made me wasn't the mix of wine and club soda I expected. Instead, he dropped a couple of lemon slices in a glass, topped them with a couple dashes of bitters, a liqueur, and ice, then poured a sparkling rosé over it. He put the glass on my coaster and waited for me to try it.

I took a tentative sip. To my surprise, I loved it.

I didn't even have to say anything. Tommy saw my reaction and smiled. "Told you you were a sparkling rosé girl. Just let me know if you need anything else, Fran." He patted the bar and walked off to help someone else.

"Francesca?"

I froze. *That was not Mike*, I told myself. *Mike is not here.* But whoever it was apparently knew me. I turned around slowly.

Mike sighed. "I was afraid that was you."

"Good to see you, too, Mike." I took a casual sip of my rosé spritzer.

He gestured at the barstool next to me, and I nodded. He swung his leg over the stool and sat down. "So, what are you doing here?"

"Matt and I thought we'd get away for a romantic weekend before tourist season got started. What about you?"

Tommy walked up to ask Mike what he wanted. I

waited until he had his beer and then asked again. "What about you?"

Mike looked at me out of the corner of his eye and didn't say anything.

I looked around in case he was trying to be discreet, but aside from Tommy and a solitary man at the other end of the bar, we were the only people in earshot. "Michael?"

He looked into his beer and muttered something.

"What was that?" I asked, leaning in.

His word came out as a growl. "Same."

I stared at him in shocked silence. "With… Sandra?" I finally managed to choke out. Mike and his wife, Sandra, had been separated for a few months now, but I knew Mike was hoping they'd be able to work things out. And I was hoping that if he was there for a romantic weekend, it was with her. I was rooting for them.

He looked at me with an expression of pure indig-nation. "Yes, with Sandra. Who else would I be here with?"

"Well, I was hoping it was her, but…" I shrugged.

He rolled his eyes and went back to his beer.

I was taking another sip of my spritzer when I remembered that I thought I saw him down in the spa while we were waiting to be let out.

"Hey, you weren't down in the spa earlier, were you? With the police?"

"Yes," he growled.

"But this isn't your jurisdiction."

"Nope."

I looked at him and waited, eyebrows raised.

He sighed. "Sandra and I were in the spa café when they found the body. I've been to enough crime scenes to know that the last thing people are concerned about is preserving evidence. Most of them are just interested in getting an eyeful."

I cringed at the crassness of it but knew it was probably true.

"I showed my badge at the desk and secured the scene. Local guys looped me in when they got here."

"You took your badge to the spa with you?" For some reason, that was the strangest part of the story for me.

"Of course." He looked at me like it was ridiculous that I would think he didn't.

"Do you have it on you now?"

In less than a blink of an eye, he reached back, pulled his wallet out, and flipped it open for me to see his badge. I was afraid of what he would do if I asked if he had his gun on him too.

He put his wallet away, took another swallow from his beer glass, and shifted uncomfortably on his barstool, then cleared his throat. "Actually, uh, Franny, I'm glad you're here."

I thought it was probably the first time he'd ever said he was happy to see me.

"I need you to do me a favor."

"Sure. What do you need?" I thought he probably wanted me to pick out which spa treatment he should book for Sandra or which treat he should get her from the French bakery.

"I need you to find out who killed that girl."

Chapter 7

I STARED at Mike in shocked silence. There was no way he'd really just asked me to investigate a murder. Not after he'd spent the last year or so telling me to mind my own business when I'd somehow managed to get myself involved in one murder case after another.

"You can't be serious. How many beers have you had exactly?" I leaned over to sniff him, but he swatted me away before I could catch a whiff of anything other than a faint hint of soap.

Mike rubbed his hand back and forth across his forehead. "Look, Fran, I know I usually tell you to let the police do their jobs, but this is different."

"Why? Because it's not your case?"

He shrugged. "Partly. But also because I need this to get wrapped up quickly, and as much as it annoys me, you're good at this stuff."

"Thank you," I muttered reflexively. It wasn't exactly a glowing endorsement, but it was high praise coming from Mike. High praise that momentarily distracted me from the first part of his sentence. "Wait, why do you need it wrapped up quickly?"

He grimaced and rubbed the back of his neck.

I wondered if the pain in it was caused by me or something else—or maybe someone else.

"Sandra—" he started then stopped to rub his neck some more. "This weekend was supposed to be kind of a fresh start for us—" His eyes went from the bar top to the bottles of liquor on the wall across from us to the ceiling. Anywhere but to me. "We have a couples massage booked—"

"So do we!"

He looked at me like I'd shared something deeply personal or possibly disgusting. After a second, he shook his head and looked back down at the bar top. "Local guys said the spa will be closed for at least a day, maybe longer depending on what evidence they do or don't find and how the investigation goes."

"When's your massage scheduled for?" Ours was Sunday morning. I wondered if the spa would still be closed by then. I hoped not. I was really looking forward to it.

Mike looked at his watch. "This time tomorrow." He took another swallow of his beer.

"And you don't think the police will have it figured out by then?"

"I don't even know if they'll be done processing the crime scene by then. Do you know how many fingerprints there are down there? They keep it clean, but—" He stopped and shook his head. "I don't know what I'm going to do, Franny."

"The restaurants are open. You could take her for a romantic dinner, maybe go for a walk outside. Didn't I see that there's a piano bar somewhere too?"

He shook his head. "I already planned to do all that. I had the whole weekend all planned out. But the massage was supposed to be the big romantic couple thing. But with this girl turning up dead—she thinks it's a bad sign. Like the universe is telling her we shouldn't get back together."

Even if I hadn't been able to hear the pain in his voice, I would have known he was upset by the way he was working his jaw.

I hated to ask it, but I had to: "Will she change her mind if they catch whoever did it?"

He turned his hands palms up and shrugged. "I don't know. But it's my only chance."

I nodded slowly, wondering as I did if there was anything I could do to help the investigation along and whether it would actually make a difference. One thing I did know was that I would try, for Mike and Sandra's sake. They'd been together almost twenty years, since we were all back in high school. I remembered them back then—Mike quiet and serious but a good enough athlete to letter in three sports and

Sandra his opposite, bubbly and friendly, with long, shiny sandy-blond hair that swung as she bounced down the halls. They'd always been polar opposites but in the best possible way, where every one of her strengths complemented his weaknesses and vice versa. And their two kids were little mini-mes, except with opposite personalities. I didn't want to see Mike and Sandra break up, for their kids' sake and for their own.

"Okay," I said quietly.

"Thanks," he replied, stone-faced and without meeting my eye. It was the most effusive expression of gratitude I could expect from him. He slugged back the rest of his beer and stood up. "I better get back up to the room. She wanted some alone time to take a bath, but I don't want her to think I wandered off."

"I'll walk with you."

Tommy appeared instantly with the slips to charge our drinks to our rooms. We signed, thanked him, and headed back toward the lobby.

"Which way's your room?"

He pointed to the right.

"Ours too."

He paused by the lobby elevator.

"If we use the other one, we can go by the patisserie. Have you been in there yet?" I wondered if maybe he and Sandra had managed to catch the girl who worked there. Of course, if they'd been by and the counter had been as empty as when Matt and I stopped in, I knew that Mike would have had little patience with it.

"The patty-what?" he asked.

"Patisserie. The French bakery."

He shook his head as he ambled alongside me with his hands in his pockets. "Sounds fancy."

I wasn't sure whether saying that it was would be a selling point with Mike. He was the primary consumer of drip coffee at my café after all. Drip coffee that he drank piping hot and black, of course. I ignored the comment. "You could get something to take up to Sandra. They had some really beautiful tortes and tarts when Matt and I went by earlier."

Mike raised an eyebrow.

I knew what he was asking without him even having to say anything. The eyebrow was enough. "Fancy cake and pie."

He nodded. "Told you it sounded fancy." And he smirked. Which was at least a good sign that he was agreeing to stop in to see what they had.

To my pleasant surprise, a petite brunette with a chin-length angled bob who had an overall very French vibe stood at the counter.

"*Bonjour!*" she cooed. "Welcome to the Pâtisserie Alford. I am Sophie. How can I help you?" Her English was good, but her accent was French.

I eyed the rows of macarons but figured I should get Mike taken care of first since he was likely to decide it wasn't worth it and wander off if

I spent too much time debating between the lemon- and raspberry-flavored macarons. Or chocolate and red velvet. Or vanilla bean and cookies and cream. There were lots of options, and I could see Mike getting impatient long before I made up my mind.

"We're looking for something that he can take back to his wife," I told her.

A coy smile crossed her lips. "Ah, yes, of course." She looked from Mike to me with a gleam in her eye. "Something to make *madame* a little more forgiving, *non?*"

Mike's eyebrows rose as my eyes got big.

"What?" My voice came out probably a little louder and much shriekier than I intended. I took a step away from Mike. "No, no, no, that's not what I meant! His wife is upstairs. We were just talking."

Sophie smiled. "*Mais oui.*" The look on her face said she didn't believe me. She turned to Mike, who looked like he was ready to turn around and walk out. "Your wife, she likes chocolate, *non?* Perhaps she would like an éclair. Or pain au chocolat. Or perhaps an entremets?"

Mike looked at me with wide eyes as Sophie gestured at the various confections. I was pretty sure the only one of those words he'd understood was éclair. To be fair, I only knew the others because I liked to bake.

"We also have many types of macarons if you

think she would prefer." She walked over to the macaron case. "Such pretty colors, *non*?"

Mike looked at the rainbow of cookies in the case and then back at me.

"They're almond cookies with filling," I told him.

He didn't look too sure about them, but I figured they would be a safe enough choice. Sandra could always come down later and pick out one of the rich, chocolatey pastries if she wanted to.

"She's not allergic to nuts, is she?"

He shook his head.

"Okay, let's get macarons, then." I looked at the options and decided to get her a box of six. Two chocolatey, two fruity, one vanilla, and one vanilla rose. That last one was risky, partly because rose wasn't a flavor everyone necessarily liked, but also because when it wasn't done right, it had a tendency to taste like soap. But if anyone could make a good rose macaron, it was Jacques de Gaulle.

I went ahead and picked out a box for myself too. Well, for me and Matt. I would probably share with him. Probably.

For my box, I chose the pretty purple lavender coconut, another vanilla rose with the soft pink shell, a coffee, and an espresso (so I could taste the difference), then rounded out the box with lemon in the rich yellow, and raspberry with, well, a raspberry-colored cookie shell.

Both boxes looked beautiful, but I had to stop

Sophie when she tried to put them in one bag. "No, he needs to take his to his wife in their room."

She gave me that disbelieving look again but moved the boxes into separate bags. She handed over the bags. We signed the separate slips—which took yet another reminder that neither we nor our orders were together—and we left to go back to our rooms.

"So, what are these things called again?" Mike asked as we went down the long hall toward the elevators.

"Macarons." The hall we were in was lined with conference rooms on both sides, another lounge area with a collection of scattered chairs and couches, and an art installation I wanted to come back and look at.

"Macaroons?"

I sighed Hadn't I just had this conversation with Matt? "Maca*rons*," I enunciated, emphasizing the key last syllable that differentiated the name of the French sandwich-style almond cookies from the sweetened piles of coconut.

Mike's eyebrow predictably rose in an expression that somehow communicated that he expected that there was more to the story. I had a feeling it was incredibly useful when he was interviewing suspects back in Cape Bay.

"Well, some people do call them macaroons, but that's incredibly confusing because they're nothing alike, so now more people are using the French pronunciation and calling these macarons to cut down on the confusion. Which is good because you'd hate to order a macaroon and get the shredded coconut kind when you were expecting these."

"Would I?" Mike punched the button for the elevator.

He had a point. "Okay, maybe *you* wouldn't, but normal people would."

I actually got a chuckle out of him. We stepped onto the elevator.

"Which floor?" he asked, his finger hovering over the number panel.

"Three."

He groaned and punched the three and nothing else.

"You're on the third floor too?"

"Maybe Sandra was right about this trip being a bad idea."

We got off the elevator and both turned right. Mike groaned again. I could see his exasperation growing with every door we passed. A little more than three quarters of the way down the hallway, he stopped at a door and watched as I walked two more doors down to my room.

I held my key card over the lock but didn't put it in yet. Mike was still watching me. "What?"

"I'm waiting to see if that's really your room or if you're just messing with me."

I grinned, slid the key into the slot, and opened the door.

He rolled his eyes and unlocked his door. "Hey, Fran?" he said just as I stepped one foot into my room. "If you need any help with that thing we talked about, let me know. I might be able to get some information. Professional courtesy."

I nodded and thanked him then stepped into my room, where I found, lying on the table in the entryway, a macaron box from the patisserie downstairs just like the one I had in my bag.

Chapter 8

"DID YOU GET ME MACARONS?"

Matt appeared from around the corner (our room was big enough and fancy enough that it had corners you could disappear around) with a big grin on his face. "Yup! I looked at the room service menu and realized you could order from the bakery, so I just called down and had them delivered. I thought it might be easier than trying to catch somebody working in there."

I slowly raised the bag I was holding.

Matt looked at it curiously for a moment. "I guess you found someone working there?"

"Yup, and you'll never guess what else I found. Or who, I should say."

"Who?"

I grabbed the box from the table. "Let's go sit and eat these, and I'll tell you all about it."

Matt, good natured as he was, shrugged and followed me and my two boxes of macarons back around the corner and over to the sitting area. I sat down, put both boxes on the table, and opened them.

Matt sat next to me and leaned over my shoulder to look at the boxes. "I didn't know what kind you'd like, so I just asked for the most popular ones."

"Works for me." If we had any duplicates, those would be the obvious ones to share with Matt.

I opened the box he'd ordered first. I smiled down at the multi-colored cookies. It was one of my favorite things about macarons—all the beautiful colors and flavors they came in. Lucky for me, they'd included a key so I didn't have to blindly guess the flavors.

I looked from the key to the box and pointed. "The green one must be pistachio, yellow is lemon, dark pink and brown is strawberry chocolate, brown is chocolate, and white is vanilla bean." I was surprised that there weren't too many duplicates from my box, especially since I didn't think my selections had been that out there. Well, except for the lavender coconut. That one was definitely out there. But that's why I wanted to try it. Getting two different coffee flavors was probably unusual too. "Which one do you want to try?"

"What kinds did you get?"

I opened up the second box and told him the flavors. I definitely had no competition for the two floral flavors.

"I'll stick with vanilla to start." He pulled the vanilla cookie out and bit into it.

I watched him as his expression went from thoughtful to pleased.

"It's good. Interesting. But good."

True to my nature, I pulled out the espresso-flavored one from the box I'd chosen. The shell had a slight crunch as I bit down into it that gave way to the chewy inside. The espresso flavor was perfect. Whatever they'd used to achieve it had worked. It wasn't bitter at all but had all the rich flavor of a perfectly roasted shot of espresso. I moaned a little and leaned back on the couch.

"That good, huh?" Matt asked, one side of his mouth twitching in a smirk.

"That good." I took another bite and let the flavor roll around in my mouth. It really was delicious. One more bite and it was done. I mentally debated whether to have another one. I knew I really shouldn't, but they were so delicious. I sat up to look in the boxes and realized Matt was already working on his second cookie. "What if I wanted that one?"

He held what was left of the chocolate macaron out to me. "You can have the rest."

"No thanks." I picked the vanilla rose instead. It had the same perfect crisp and chewy texture, the warm taste of vanilla, and the slightest hint of rose—just enough to detect it and nowhere near enough to taste soapy.

When Matt reached for another one, I swatted his hand. "Don't we have a dinner reservation soon?"

"Not for another hour." He reached for the box again.

I closed both of them and moved them to the other side of the room. "Nope, saving the rest for later."

He mock-pouted but pulled me onto his lap as soon as I came back to the couch. "You really can't make those?"

"I *can*. I just don't want to. Not for the café anyway. They're not hard, but they're finicky. And I have enough to worry about with the café anyway."

Immediately, everything that had been on my mind back in Cape Bay came rushing back, and I wondered what I'd been thinking to even agree to come on this trip. I had too much to do, too much to figure out. I felt confident that the café was in good hands with Sammy, but she was there to keep it running, not to do all the budgeting and planning that I'd been working on before I left.

"We're not thinking about the café this weekend, remember?" He kissed me on the neck, and I forgot a little bit about the café. "We're thinking about us—" Another kiss, and the café faded away a little more. "And relaxation—" I started to wonder what I'd been so worked up about after all. "And whether you can make me some of those cookies when we get home."

I giggled. "I think I can do that."

"Good," he murmured and kissed me again, a long, slow kiss that banished every last thought of Cape Bay and the café from my mind.

An hour later, we went downstairs for our dinner reservation at one of the hotel's fancy restaurants.

We were seated at a cozy table by the windows, where we could watch the sun set over the mountains. It was beautiful, and the food was delicious. By the time we wandered out after three courses and almost two hours, all I wanted to do was go up to our room and curl up in that luxurious-looking bed with Matt. And that's where we were headed when Matt reminded me of the unpleasant events of the afternoon.

"Did you hear the waiter tell one of the other tables that they closed the spa down to investigate that girl's death? Hopefully they get everything figured out and open it back up before our massage."

I realized I'd forgotten to tell Matt about my conversation with Mike. And that I was supposed to help him out by investigating the murder. In fact, I'd been so distracted by the macarons that I'd forgotten to tell him I'd seen Mike at all. It seemed like a weird moment to bring it up now, but it would just get weirder if I waited longer.

"That probably sounded pretty shallow, huh? Sorry."

I looked up at Matt, a little confused.

"You weren't saying anything, so I thought—"

"Oh! No, I was just thinking about something."

He raised his eyebrows. "That sounds like trouble." He knew me too well.

"I wouldn't say *trouble*."

"Of course you wouldn't."

I stopped by one of the chairs scattered in the long hallway to the elevator. "Remember how I thought I saw Mike and Sandra?"

He rubbed a hand across his face and through his hair. "Are we on that again? I thought we weren't going to think about Cape Bay this weekend."

I ignored him. "I ran into Mike in the lobby lounge this afternoon while you were sleeping."

Matt blinked at me for a second with his eyebrows raised, then he smiled. "You're messing with me."

"Nope. Dead serious." His eyebrows went up again, and I cringed. "Sorry, bad word choice."

"And here I was apologizing for being insensitive." He sighed. "So you saw Mike, huh?"

"Yup. He and Sandra are here trying to patch things up."

"Well, that's good. Hope they can work it out." He turned to start heading for the elevator, realized I wasn't following him, and turned back around. "What?" I don't think he even made an effort to put dread in his voice.

"Well..."

"Spit it out."

"Mike asked me to try to help solve the girl's murder."

Matt stared at me blankly. "Are you serious?" he asked finally.

I nodded.

"Mike? Our Mike? Mike *Stanton*? The one who's always telling you to stay out of police business. *He* asked you to investigate a murder?"

"Yup, that's the one."

"Are you sure?"

"Of course I'm sure," I said. "He and Sandra are scheduled for a couples massage tomorrow, and she thinks the murder is a bad sign, so he wants it to get wrapped up as quickly as possible."

Matt still looked skeptical.

"He said I'm good at it."

"Okay, now I know you're making things up."

"No, I'm not." I stood up from where I leaned against the chair and wrapped my arms around him. "He's seen my good work. And it's not his case this time, so he doesn't care that I'm in the way."

Matt brushed a kiss across my lips. "See, even you admit that you get in the way."

I grinned. "Never said I didn't."

He kissed me again, so soft and slow that I considered forgetting about investigating for the night and just heading upstairs. But duty won out.

"Let's go down to the lounge and get a couple after-dinner drinks. What do you say?"

Matt chuckled softly. "You just want to get to work on this."

"Maybe." I intertwined my fingers with his and started pulling him back toward the lobby. "But a nightcap would be nice, wouldn't it?"

He shook his head slowly, the smile still curling the corners of his lips up. "You're too much. You know that?"

"Yes." I smiled. "But you love me anyway."

"Yes, I do." He kissed the top of my head and let me lead him toward the lobby.

Chapter 9

THE LOBBY LOUNGE was alive with activity when we got there. A jazz quartet played in the corner by the piano, and several couples danced on the parquet floor as the band played what sounded distinctly like a cover of a popular pop song from a few years ago. I tried not to giggle as the singer scatted the rap portion of the song.

Matt shook his head as the singer shooby-doo'd a line I remembered being edited out of the radio version of the song and headed for the bar.

"Look!" I pointed excitedly at the coffee bar. "The barista's actually there!"

"Seems like an odd time to show up to work."

"I don't care. I'm going to get a cup of coffee."

"You're never going to sleep tonight."

I shrugged and made a beeline for the coffee bar. "It'll be fine."

Matt went to the bar to order something that, admittedly, was probably a more appropriate drink for the time of the night. But still, there was coffee, and I wanted some. Tommy had been a good sport about fumbling through making a macchiato by following my directions, but I was excited to see what the real barista could do.

"Hi!" I said cheerfully as I walked up to the counter.

The barista sauntered over to me and leaned against the counter, his hands spread wide. "What can I get for you?" The way he said it was more like a come-on than a request to take my order.

"What's your favorite?" I, of course, knew what I wanted—another macchiato with those Ecuadorian beans—but I always liked to ask that question when I went to a new coffee shop or had someone new helping me. I felt like it gave me a good idea of who they were as a barista and what I could expect from whatever kind of drink I did end up getting. And sometimes their favorite sounded really good, and I actually did get it.

He gave me a look that was more a leer than a normal smile. "A green eye. You know what that is?"

I nodded.

"It's a black coffee with three shots of espresso."

"I know that."

He actually winked at me. "Of course you do."

"I'll have a macchiato. With the Ecuadorian beans

if you have any more ready," I said dryly. I didn't want to encourage him.

He raised his eyebrow and smirked at me. "The Ecuadorian beans, huh? They're a little strong. Pretty pricey too. We charge extra for them. Are you sure you don't just want the kind you're used to?" He gestured at a grocery store blend behind him.

I swallowed down my instant irritation at his assumption that I couldn't handle a strong cup of coffee and wouldn't appreciate the high-end blend. I smiled politely however. "Yes, I'm sure."

He shrugged. "If you say so. But if you don't like it when you get it, I'll make you a new one with the regular stuff. On the house." He winked at me, and I felt my stomach churn at his attitude. He grabbed a cup. "Right, a latte macchiato." He reached for the milk to steam. "You know why it's called a macchiato? It's Italian."

"An *espresso* macchiato," I corrected.

"Yeah, there's espresso in it."

"No, I want an espresso macchiato, not a latte macchiato." Actually, a latte macchiato would have been a good choice for that time of night since it was more milk than coffee, but I resented his assumption. I could see in his eyes that he assumed that since I was a girl, I couldn't possibly want the stronger drink.

He raised his eyebrows with an amused smirk and went ahead and said it. "You know that's pretty strong, right? It's mostly espresso—"

"It's espresso marked with milk. I know. That's why it's called a macchiato. Macchiato means 'marked' in Italian."

He looked at me with something between annoyance and disgust. "Well, aren't you a smart cookie."

I gritted my teeth at his impressing level of condescension. "I have some experience."

"Go to a lot of coffee shops, huh?"

I took a slow, deep breath to keep myself from saying anything I'd regret. Even after I did, I still wanted to say something to put him in his place. He could only be a little bit more than ten years younger than me—in his early twenties, I guessed—but I still wanted to snap at him to have a little respect for his elders.

Fortunately, Tommy saved us both from making a scene.

"Hey, Carrick, this is the lady I was telling you about," he said, walking over to the edge of the bar and nodding in my direction.

Carrick looked from Tommy to me. "Oh, the one who runs the little coffee shop?"

"I own it," I said through clenched teeth. "It's been in my family for over fifty years."

"Oh, well, that explains it." He chuckled and went back to making my drink—steaming the milk for way too long, I might add. "You learned about coffee from Daddy."

I was ready to climb across the counter. For one

thing, I didn't think my father had ever set foot inside Antonia's—he'd taken off too fast. But for another, what did it matter if I learned about coffee from my mother and grandparents? I knew my stuff no matter where or how I'd learned it.

"Stop being a jerk, Carrick." Tommy looked annoyed. At least I wasn't the only one. He looked at me. "Tell him off if you need to, Fran. No one will blame you. In fact, everyone appreciates when someone puts him in his place."

Carrick glared at Tommy and sullenly went about pulling the espresso for my drink. He'd now spent more time mouthing off to me than it would have taken to just make the drink.

Tommy ignored Carrick and looked me in the eye. "I'm serious. And if he doesn't lay off, you come tell me, okay?"

I nodded. I wasn't sure that I would ever either tell off Carrick or tattle on him to Tommy, but at least I knew I wasn't the only one he treated like dirt.

Matt walked over, carrying a highball glass filled with a brown liquid—whiskey, I guessed—over ice. He slipped his arm around my waist and brushed a kiss across my temple. "Everything going okay over here?"

Carrick looked at us out of the corner of his eye. I wondered if he was more afraid of Matt than he was of me.

I looked dead at him. "Mm-hmm. The barista here was just making my espresso macchiato."

Carrick's nostrils flared. "I'm a baris*to*, not a baris*ta*."

I raised my eyebrows. "Baristo" was not a word.

"Yeah, it's like how a male ballet dancer is called a ballerino, not a ballerina. In Spanish, when a person is a male, you change the A at the end of a word to an O."

That was true, but neither of those words were Spanish.

"It's a really common mistake. A lot of people make it. You shouldn't feel bad that you didn't know that."

Matt's arm tightened around my waist. I glanced over at Tommy, who I could tell was half listening. With my teeth clenched tight, I said, "I didn't know it because it's not true."

Carrick laughed as he somehow *still* worked on making my drink. It should not have taken that long. "I understand why you'd think that, but it really is baristo—"

"No. It's. Not."

"Yeah, actually, it is."

"No, it's not, Carrick." Tommy whipped a towel over his shoulder and came over to stand near me at the coffee bar. "Don't be a moron. You know that baristo's not a word, and it's not going to become one just because you keep saying it is."

Carrick pouted and finally poured the milk into my espresso that had to already be a little cooler than it should be.

"And of all people," Tommy continued, "why would you try to tell her that when you know she owns a coffee shop?"

Carrick pushed the drink over to me sullenly and without saying a word. I could tell at a glance that he'd gone too heavy on the milk. It was more mixed than marked with milk. Normally, I wouldn't say anything, especially when it was a high-quality blend like this that I hated to see go to waste, but...

"This has too much milk." I pushed it back across the counter.

"How do you know? You haven't even tried it." Carrick slid it toward me again.

"How do you know if you put the right amount in without trying it?"

Matt and Tommy burst out laughing as Carrick's face twitched. He snatched the cup back and poured it out, then brought it back over to the espresso machine.

"A clean cup, please." I smiled sweetly.

Matt leaned on the counter to support himself as he cracked up. Tommy turned away, presumably to keep his coworker from seeing exactly how hard he was laughing at his expense. If Carrick was looking though, Tommy's shaking shoulders would have given him away.

Carrick put my cup in the dirty dish bin and got out a new one. This time, I watched as he made my fresh drink at a normal pace. He passed it across the counter when it was finished, and I looked down into the cup.

"Color looks good." I sniffed it, putting on a little bit of a show to demonstrate that I wasn't going to be a pushover, and nodded that the smell met my approval. I was tempted to swish my first sip around my mouth and then spit it out like I was at a wine tasting, but I resisted the urge and swallowed it down—although I did swish it around a little, but that was because I wanted to savor the rich flavor.

Matt and Tommy watched me a little too intently. I would have liked to think that they were just concerned about whether I would like it, but I was pretty sure they were both hoping it would be terrible and I would completely lose my cool on Carrick. While Matt had only just met him, I got the feeling that Tommy had been waiting a long time to see Carrick get his comeuppance.

As much as I would have liked to provide their entertainment for the evening, I wasn't going to lie. I smiled as I put the cup down. "Very good."

Matt and Tommy's disappointment was visible. They reacted like their team had missed a score or a point or whatever in a sports game. Well, they didn't yell or anything, but they definitely would have liked to see my reaction if the macchiato hadn't been good. Unfortunately for them, it was perfection.

Carrick, for his part, smiled smugly, like he knew it would be all along. It was kind of an odd reaction for someone who had literally just screwed up the exact same drink, but based on what little I already knew about him, it wasn't surprising.

I stuck my hand out across the counter. "Truce?" I didn't want to declare one, but I remembered that I was supposed to be investigating the murder for Mike. As much as I hated to admit it, Carrick could have some information about it that could prove useful.

He looked at me suspiciously but finally reached out and took my hand. "Truce." The smug smile back on his face, it was obvious he thought he was doing me a favor by agreeing even though I had clearly been the one to come out on top since I'd gotten him to remake my coffee the right way.

Seeing that the action was over for the time being, Tommy went back to the bar to take care of his customers. Matt pulled up a barstool next to me and sat down.

As I sipped my drink, I watched Carrick move around the coffee bar, fiddling with things. I had to figure out how to get him talking. For lack of a better idea and because he didn't seem like the type who cared much for social niceties, I decided to just go for it.

"So I guess you knew Gina?" I was glad I'd overheard her name. I would have felt much more awkward asking if he knew "that girl who got killed."

A strange look passed over his face like a shadow. "Yeah, I knew her."

"It must be hard for you to keep working when your friend just died."

He shrugged. "We weren't really friends." But he looked uncomfortable.

Matt looked at me with an expression that said he wasn't sure what I was doing. Neither was I, but I knew I had to get some useful information. Mike was depending on me.

"Oh really? Was she not the friendly type?"

"She was fine."

This wasn't going well. I decided to take a different approach. "We were actually down in the spa when they found her. Everyone down there seemed pretty upset."

He tried to hide it, but I could see that this got Carrick's attention. He wiped the already-clean counter with a rag. "Oh yeah? Who all was down there?"

"I only caught a couple of names," I said as casually as I could. "Noelle was one. And Amber. She's the one who found her."

Carrick nodded thoughtfully, which raised my curiosity about why he wanted to know who was down there.

"Do you know them?" It was a stupid question, but I wanted to keep him talking.

"Yeah, I pretty much know everyone around here. It's not a big place."

And you have such a winning personality. I had the self-restraint not to say it out loud. Barely.

I glanced around like I was making sure no one could overhear and leaned in. "So, do you have any idea who could have killed her? Did she have any enemies? Did anyone have it in for her?"

He raised an eyebrow and looked at me out of the corner of his eye, making me wonder if I'd gone too far. But apparently, he didn't think so, or at least if he did, he wasn't showing it. "I wouldn't know."

"Who would?"

He looked straight at me. "What, are you with the cops or something?"

Matt snorted into his whiskey. "No, she's just nosy."

"Shut up," I said, swatting at him. I didn't know if he'd said it with the intention of helping me out or not, but I could see it working. I tried to look casual and disinterested. "Just curious is all."

Carrick smirked at me yet again. "You're one of those types, huh? Morbid fascination with death? I bet you're one of those looky-loos who holds up traffic because you're trying to get a look at an accident."

I was not, and I resented the suggestion, but if it got him talking, I was willing to let him think so. I shrugged and tried to look embarrassed. "You know, I'm just… curious."

He shook his head and looked superior. "Well, I don't judge."

I doubted that.

"If you really want to know the dirt on Gina, you need to talk to her friends." Carrick began pulling shots of espresso into a cup.

"So who were her friends?"

"The spa girls."

"And where can I find them?"

He looked at Matt like he was trying to see if Matt was hearing my apparent stupidity too. "In the spa."

I tried to squash down my impatience. I was pretty sure he was being deliberately difficult and that he was going to make me drag every single solitary piece of information out of him one by one. "So I should just go down to the spa and start asking them about Gina?"

He laughed. "Well, no, they're not going to talk to you while they're at *work*."

I stifled a sigh. "So where do they hang out when they're not at work?" It was probably what I should have asked in the first place, but I didn't think he'd take quite so much pleasure in talking down to me.

"Home." He chuckled like it was funny.

"Anywhere else?"

"There's a spot they hang out on their breaks out by the loading bay. Just follow the noise."

"Of the trucks at the loading docks?"

"No, of their yammering. You can hear it a mile away."

I rolled my eyes and picked up my coffee cup. "Thanks." I tried to keep the snarkiness I felt out of my voice. "Come on, let's go sit over by the band," I said to Matt.

I smiled to myself as we crossed the lounge to where the jazz quartet had continued working their way through the pop hits of five years ago. Despite Carrick's efforts to be difficult, I had a good idea of who I wanted to talk to next.

It was too late that night to go in search of "the spa girls," as Carrick had called them, or at least that's what Matt told me. I had to admit he was probably right. It had been several hours since the police closed down the spa, and even if they hadn't, the spa's regular hours were long since over. No one from the spa had any reason to still be hanging around. I couldn't say I minded too much since there were macarons in the room. And Matt.

So we went back upstairs, where we found, to my amazement, that the hotel had provided turndown service. The blankets were pulled partway back on both sides of the bed, and there was a chocolate on each of our pillows. A notecard left on the bed said, "Turndown Service provided by Bertina." The house-keeper's name was written in what I could only assume was her own handwriting, which made me wonder if she carried the cards around already filled out or if she borrowed a pen in each room. Pre-filled out seemed more efficient.

I wondered how she'd known that we were out of the room or if it even mattered. Maybe Bertina would have come by even if we were sitting on the couch watching TV and just turned down the bed while we cuddled and watched a romantic comedy. Okay, Matt probably would have been watching the Celtics, and I would have been playing on my phone, but the principle was the same. Or maybe the housekeeping staff had checked our dinner reservation and knew when we'd be gone. I wasn't sure which idea I liked better—or which creeped me out more.

I took a long hot bath while Matt—obviously—watched the Celtics play against some other team I didn't recognize. Not that I recognized many basketball teams. Or really any other than the home team. I couldn't help but think that that would have been an awkward time for Bertina to come in. I was glad she somehow sensed that she should come earlier.

As I eventually went to sleep that night, I thought about Gina's murder and how sad it was. At least I had made some progress in figuring out who I needed to talk to. No doubt, Mike would be pleased the next time I talked to him.

I was wrong. He was not pleased.

Chapter 10

I WAS sound asleep when the ringing of my cell phone woke me up. I wanted to ignore it, but despite my minimal level of consciousness, I realized that the room was still dark. The only reason for someone to be calling me when it was still dark was if it was Sammy telling me there was something wrong at the café.

I barely looked at the phone as I hit the button to answer the call and held it to my ear. "Hello?" I croaked.

"It's me," a voice said, barely above a whisper. It didn't sound like Sammy, but she wasn't much of a whisperer. She was far too enthusiastic for that. "Where are you?"

"What?" I still wasn't awake enough to make any sense of what was going on. Why was someone calling me in the middle of the night, asking me where I was?

"I'm in bed."

"With the case! And why aren't you awake? It's nine o'clock in the morning!"

Something in my brain recognized the voice, but it wasn't Sammy's. It was a man's. I felt the bed next to me. Matt was still there, and by the way he swatted at my hand as it patted his face, I didn't think he was calling me from over there. Was it someone with the hotel maybe? But why would they call my cell?

"Mike?"

"Of course it's Mike! Who did you think it was?" Despite his hushed voice, I could hear his annoyance.

"Why are you calling me in the middle of the night, asking about the case?"

"It's nine a.m.!"

I rolled over to peer out one of the windows. The tiniest crack of light showed through. Of course. Matt had closed the blackout shades so we could sleep in after our late night. Neither of us had expected Mike to call first thing.

Matt shifted in the bed, and I realized that my conversation was waking him up.

"Hold on," I whispered to Mike. I slipped out of bed and wrapped myself in the fluffy white robe the hotel provided. I crept across the room, only tripping once over the coffee table. I managed to stifle my yelp and made it out to the balcony. "Okay, I can talk now."

He sighed, and I got the feeling that I was

annoying him. I didn't care. He was the one who woke me up.

"So where are you?" he asked.

"On the balcony now."

"*With the case.*"

"Oh, right." I pulled my robe a little bit tighter. "It's going well! I talked to the barista in the lobby lounge last night and found out that Gina was closest with the spa girls. I'm going to try to talk to them today." I deliberately called Carrick a barista. Even if I thought it was a word, there was no way I was going to call him a baristo. It was stupid.

"Okay, what else?"

I tried to think of what else I had learned. "The bartender seemed upset about her death."

"Okay." He paused. "What else?"

"Um, the barista is kind of a jerk?"

"About the case, Fran!"

"That's about it."

There was a long pause before Mike said, "That's it?"

"Yeah, so far. Like I said, I'm going to try to talk to the spa girls today and see if they have any ideas on who could have killed Gina."

"That's all you've found out?" The surprise in his voice was obvious even though he was still speaking very quietly. I guessed that it was because he was trying to keep Sandra from hearing, either because she was still asleep or because he didn't want her to know that he had asked me to get involved.

"It hasn't even been a day, Mike."

"Our spa appointment is in less than six hours, Fran." He had a point.

"Okay, I'll try to go talk to them."

"Now?"

"If I can find them."

Nothing from Mike's end. I had a feeling he wasn't used to getting pushback from the people working on his investigations. Unfortunately for him, he wasn't my boss. But I did want to help him.

"I'll find them," I said. I wasn't sure how, but I would figure it out.

He begrudgingly accepted it with a promise from me that I would check back in with him in two hours. He wanted it to just be one hour, but I reminded him that I still needed to get dressed. I didn't think he cared, but he agreed to two hours anyway.

We said goodbye, and I slipped back inside. Matt was still sound asleep. I grabbed some clothes from my bag and got dressed quickly in the bathroom. I scribbled down a note for Matt and left it on the bedside table, then slipped out of the room.

I half expected Mike to be waiting outside his room to make sure I left like I said I would. He wasn't there, but I realized that he could have been watching through his peephole without me knowing. I smiled and waved as I walked by the door, just in case.

Downstairs, I looked longingly at one of the restaurants when I passed it. It was the one with the amazing-looking brunch menu, and I'd been hoping to have a nice breakfast there, maybe even with a mimosa or two. But Mike was counting on me, so I told myself I'd just stop in at the bakery and grab a croissant.

I shouldn't have been surprised that the patisserie counter was unattended, but I was. I briefly considered helping myself and leaving a five on the counter but decided that probably wasn't a good idea. I'd just have to be hungry.

Garrett, the manager, was at the front desk as I walked by. I waved and said good morning, but he ignored me. So much for the good customer service he was supposedly so concerned about. I was sure Whitney would have at least said hello.

I stepped outside and looked around for where the loading dock was. I had no idea if the spa girls would be there, but it was my best bet. Either that or go down to the spa itself, which was probably still roped off with police tape. It seemed like a long shot that the girls would be at the hotel at all today, but I had to try.

I didn't see any signs of where the loading dock was, so I just took a wild guess and turned right. Even if it would have been shorter to go the other way, I'd get to it eventually. Unless Carrick was lying about its existence altogether, but I didn't think he was. A hotel this size had to have somewhere to get its deliveries.

Right actually turned out to be the right way to go. I found the loading dock about halfway down the side of the building, and just beyond that, slightly blocked off by a small grove of trees, a small group of girls sat around chatting. They were scattered among a bench and a couple of chairs, with another girl sitting on the ground. With a couple of them dressed all in white, I had a good feeling that they were the spa girls—or at least some of them. Hopefully ones who knew something about Gina.

I started toward them, not sure of how I was going to strike up a conversation with them. "Hey, don't mind me. I'm just a stranger coming up to talk to you about your dead friend" didn't seem like it was going to be my best bet. And they all looked to be at least ten, maybe fifteen, years younger than me— college students or recent graduates. Not the people I had the most in common with now that I was in my midthirties and, admittedly, not as cool as I used to be, if I could even really say that I was ever cool. It was doubtful.

I considered it a stroke of luck then that, as I got closer, I realized I recognized all of them. Whitney from the front desk, dressed in all black, sat on a boulder wedged into the slight swell of ground that, combined with the grove of trees, made me under-stand why they used this as their break spot—it was out of the way and really hard to find if you didn't know where to look.

In a chair slightly apart from the other girls sat Sophie, her sleek black bob tossed back and a cigarette dangling from her fingers. That couldn't possibly be good for her sense of taste, an important trait for a baker. Maybe she didn't care though. Working the counter of a bakery didn't necessarily mean she had any interest in actually baking. She didn't seem to have any interest in doing her job either, but that was neither here nor there. I realized this must have been where she spent all her time instead of being at the counter of the bakery when I wanted a croissant.

On the bench sat the two girls in white—the spa girls I wanted to talk to. And despite the fact that I'd only spent twenty minutes in the spa and they probably had dozens of workers, I recognized these two. The one with her curly hair in a ponytail was Noelle, our tour guide in the spa. And next to her, examining her long shiny chestnut hair for split ends, was Amber, the spa technician who had stumbled screaming out of the treatment room when she found Gina's body.

I still hadn't come up with a clever way to join their group, so I decided I was just going to have to walk up and act like I belonged—the classic method of someone who wasn't necessarily doing what she was supposed to do.

They didn't notice me until I was just a few yards away, but when they did, their heads turned in unison toward me. It was almost kind of creepy the way all four of their heads swiveled as one. I tried to ignore it and kept moving toward them with what was probably a really cheesy smile plastered on my face.

"Hi, guys!" I said cheerfully when I got close enough.

"Hi," most of them said back uneasily. Apparently, hotel guests didn't often crash their break time. Sophie was the only one who didn't greet me. She just looked at me disdainfully before taking a long drag of her cigarette and exhaling the smoke in my direction. She seemed like such a lovely person.

I focused on Whitney. She was the closest to me, and I knew she'd recognized me and Matt the day before when we passed her in the hall. "I was just out for a walk, and I heard you guys talking and thought I'd come over and say hello."

The three that weren't openly ignoring me said hello again. Sophie just arched one of her perfectly groomed eyebrows a little higher.

I stood there smiling silently in hopes that one of them would start to feel awkward and say something that would give me an opening to start talking to them.

Whitney was the one who broke. "Do you want to sit down?" She gestured at the open chair. Noelle gave Whitney a subtle but unmistakable "what are you doing?" look. Whitney shrugged.

"Sure!" I grabbed the chair and pulled it over

closer before one of them could find a way to cancel the invitation.

Whitney, still the one most uncomfortable with the silence, smiled at me, a forced, put-upon smile that I read right through without caring. "So, you checked in yesterday, right?"

"Sure did!" I beamed at all of them. They all smiled hesitantly back except for Sophie, who rolled her eyes and looked away.

"I'm sorry about all the…" Whitney hesitated. "…*events* yesterday."

I had my opening. I nodded sadly. "I was down in the spa yesterday when—" I waved my hand so I didn't have to say it. They knew what I meant. "Noelle was giving me and my boyfriend a tour."

Noelle looked up and smiled weakly.

"Oh, so you were right there!" Whitney looked faintly surprised.

Amber finally looked away from her split ends and over at me like she wasn't sure if I was telling the truth. She must not have seen me. Of course, since what she had just seen was her friend's dead body, I couldn't exactly fault her for overlooking the spa guests who happened to be in the area at the time. She looked over at Noelle, who nodded again, confirming my story. Amber grabbed another section of hair to study.

"Yeah, I was." I was surprised how naturally and easily Gina's death had come up. Of course, it was the talk of the hotel. Getting the girls to tell a total stranger about who could have wanted to kill their friend might be a completely different story. "It was so —unexpected. And upsetting! And I didn't even know her. It must be so much harder for you guys."

The three civilized ones nodded. Sophie puffed away on her cigarette.

I was hoping one of them would volunteer something else, but they didn't, so I had to keep pushing and hope I didn't go too far. "And the way she died —" I shuddered, partly for show and partly because being suffocated during a mud wrap seemed particularly horrifying. "Why would anyone do something like that?"

It was mostly a rhetorical question, so I was surprised when Amber burst out for the first time. "Because he hates her, that's why!"

Noelle immediately turned to comfort her.

Whitney looked at me as though any of them had something to apologize for. "She's taking it really hard. Gina and Amber were best friends since elementary school," she said, but I was focused on Amber and what she'd said.

"Who? Who hates her?"

"Garrett!" Her voice exploded out as an anguished scream.

"The hotel manager?"

Noelle seemed to be trying to hush Amber, but

Whitney nodded at me. "He had it in for her for some reason."

"Because she wouldn't go out with him!" Amber's face was red, and fat tears rolled down her face. "He was in love with her, and he was mad that she wouldn't go out with a *jerk* and a *pig* like him! She thought he was disgusting, and he killed her!" She collapsed, sobbing into Noelle's shoulder.

Sophie was still ignoring everything and everyone around her. I looked at Whitney. She nodded slowly. "He was on her case for a while, trying to get her to go out with him, but she kept turning him down," she said quietly. "Garrett doesn't take rejection well. Or disagreement. Or anyone daring to be female, really. He's just a jerk."

"Do you think he could have killed her?" I kept my voice low too. I didn't think Amber or Noelle could hear me over the sobbing, but I didn't trust Sophie.

Whitney shifted her position on the boulder. "I don't like to think that about anyone, you know?"

"I get it. But someone obviously killed her, and if it was Garrett—"

She looked down at her silver-painted fingernails. "I don't know anybody else who hated her that much. Gina was good people, you know? Not the kind of girl to make a lot of enemies. Not the kind of girl that anyone would want to kill."

"Anyone except Garrett?"

She looked me in the eye for the first time. "He's not a good guy." Her voice came out strained and thick with emotion. There was more there than she was saying, and I didn't think it was that he brought all the girls candy and roses on Valentine's Day.

I was still looking at Whitney, with her clenched jaw and rage-filled eyes, when cell phones started blinging around me. At first, I reached for mine, but then I realized it was the only one that hadn't gone off.

Whitney was the first to get her phone out and read the message. "Shoot," or something like that, she muttered. "It's from Garrett."

Noelle and Amber looked around frantically, and even Sophie turned her head. These girls were afraid of him.

"*Under no circumstances should any hotel staffer talk to any hotel guest about the events yesterday, refer to it, or acknowledge its happening. No fraternizing. Punishable by firing,*" Whitney read. "Can you believe that? I had five people come up to me this morning wanting to talk about it. And that's not even including you." She looked at me. "At least you actually care. Everyone else just wants some hot gossip they can be the first to share. And what does Garrett expect me to do? Just look at them and say I don't know what they're talking about? Walk away? He'd fire me for that too. Geez."

"He didn't even say her name," Amber sobbed. "Or that she died! What is wrong with him? I hate him. I hate him! I should kill him. Kill him to get justice for Gina."

Noelle grabbed her shoulders. "Stop it! Don't say that. Someone will hear you!"

Whitney scrambled up and went over to Amber's other side, putting her arm around Amber's back. "You can't talk like that. I know you're angry, but you can't say stuff like that. He'll fire you if he hears you."

I noticed that neither of them were trying to argue that Garrett didn't kill Gina, just that Amber needed to be quieter about wanting revenge.

"I don't care if he fires me. I care that he killed Gina!"

They both shushed her as Sophie looked on. A door slammed somewhere in the loading dock.

"C'mon, let's get you inside." Whitney reached under Amber's arms to encourage her to get up off the bench. Noelle helped from the other side. Their arms around Amber, they started guiding her toward the door back into the hotel that had been propped open. "We have to go," Whitney said over her shoulder to me. "We can't be seen talking to you."

Sophie stood up slowly and followed them. With one last disdainful look over her shoulder, she smudged her cigarette out on the hotel's brick exterior and kicked away the doorstop. The door slammed behind her as she disappeared inside.

I grabbed my phone out of my pocket and dialed Mike's number.

Chapter 11

"GARRETT? THE HOTEL MANAGER?" Mike repeated when I told him what I'd found out from the spa girls… and Whitney. Sophie hadn't really contributed to the conversation.

"Yes, that's what they all said. Apparently, he hated her because she wouldn't go out with him." I had my hand cupped over my mouth and the phone and was speaking as quietly as I could. I was still outside near the little grove of trees, and I was keeping an eye on my surroundings as best as I could, but that didn't stop me from being nervous about someone sneaking up on me and hearing what I was telling Mike. "The things that you look for are means, motive, and opportunity, right? So he obviously had a motive—Gina refusing to go out with him. Everyone had the means because they suffocated her with one of the mud strips. And of course he had the opportunity—he's the boss. He can go wherever he wants whenever he wants, and no one thinks anything of it."

Mike was silent. I wasn't sure if he didn't believe me or couldn't hear me. "Mike?"

"Yeah, I'm just..." His voice trailed off.

I waited. "You're just...?" I finally prompted him when it didn't seem like he was going to pick his thought back up.

"What?"

"You stopped talking midsentence." I paced around the grove of trees, trying to look casual and not like I was talking to a cop about the possibility of the hotel manager being a murderer. I didn't know who could be watching.

"I did? Sorry. I just, um..." He trailed off again, and I started to wonder if I was ever going to get the rest of the sentence out of him. I was just about to give up when he picked it back up. "I'm just wondering if it's reliable information. You can't make a case based on the words of a few hysterical girls."

"Hey! Just because they're girls doesn't make them hysterical. In fact, I would say they're not girls at all. They're young women."

I could practically hear his eyes roll through the phone. "You said they were screaming and crying, didn't you? Sounds pretty hysterical to me."

"Only one of them was screaming and crying."

"The one who accused the hotel manager."

He had me there. "Well, yes, but—" I stopped my

pacing and leaned against a tree since pacing probably didn't look casual.

"Fran, that's not exactly solid evidence. You can't convict someone on the basis of the victim's upset best friend's accusation."

I sighed. I knew he was right, but I didn't like it. I snapped at him. "Well then, what do you want me to do? I did what you said and got you a name, but apparently that's not good enough." I started pacing again out of frustration. This was supposed to be a romantic weekend, and it was turning into anything but. I was spending less time with Matt than I was running around trying to solve a murder case for Mike so that *his* romantic weekend wasn't ruined.

"Ask around some more. See if anyone actually saw the guy in the area. Find out if the victim was involved in anything shady."

"And exactly how am I supposed to do any of that?"

The tone of his voice suddenly changed, and its volume dropped to where I could barely hear him over the noise of a tractor trailer backing up into the loading bay. "Look, I gotta go. You'll figure it out. You're smart. I trust you." And he hung up on me.

I took a deep breath and told myself that he probably had to hurry off the phone because Sandra had just walked in the room. From what I'd heard, their separation was caused partly because he worked all the time, so I could see why he wouldn't want her to know that he was working on Gina's murder. Although, if I wanted to get technical about it, I was the one doing the work while he shot down my theories.

But dwelling on that wasn't going to help. I had to figure out what to do next. One thought kept running through my head, but I didn't like it. I didn't want to do it. But at the same time, I knew I had to.

I started down the incline, away from the grove of trees. I took the long way around the hotel in case something else came to me. But nothing did.

As I walked back through the lobby, I realized that Tommy might have some more information. Or that awful Carrick. But I'd have to come back to them. Now that I'd decided who I should talk to, I had to do it immediately, or else I might change my mind.

And then I was there. Standing outside the patisserie, I looked to see if anyone was inside. The one time I hoped the counter would be unattended, Sophie was there, and she was even working, adjusting the arrangement of the pastry case. I took a deep breath and went inside.

"Hi, Sophie!"

She looked up with open disdain in her eyes and not a flicker of recognition.

"I don't think I ever actually introduced myself, but I'm Fran." I walked toward her with my hand out, and she gave me the most limp-fish handshake ever. And still didn't seem to recognize me. "I was just outside talking to you and the other girls," I said in an attempt to jog her memory.

No reaction.

"I was in here yesterday afternoon and bought some macarons."

"Ah, yes," she said in her French accent. "With your boyfriend."

"Yes! Wait, no!" I'd momentarily forgotten that it had been Mike with me, not Matt, when I bought the macarons. I could tell by the slight narrowing of her eyes and her hint of a smirk that my little lapse wasn't going to do me any favors in trying to convince her that Mike and I were not together. "The man you saw me with is a friend. My boyfriend and I were in here earlier in the day, but you weren't here then."

"I don't know what you're talking about. I was here all day."

I smiled sweetly. As much as I wanted to argue with her, I doubted it would do any good. "You must have just stepped into the back for a minute. Anyway, the reason I stopped in—"

"I do not go in the back. My job is here, in front." She waved her hand at the display cases.

I had a hard time believing that she literally never set foot in the back, but again, I didn't think that argument was going to get me very far.

"Oh, well—" I waved my hand with a little laugh, like it was no big deal. "Like I was saying, the reason I came by—"

I was interrupted again, but this time not by Sophie. For a second, as the hulking figure appeared behind the door to the kitchen and then walked through, I didn't register anything significant. And then I gasped.

He turned to me with a warm smile, the polar opposite of the near snarl that seemed permanently affixed to Sophie's face. "Bonjour!"

"Bonjour," I replied with what I was almost certain was probably the worst French pronunciation Jacques de Gaulle's ears had ever been cursed to hear.

"'As Sophie 'elped you?" His accent was thicker than Sophie's but smooth as chocolate.

I briefly considered telling him the truth—that Sophie had been nothing but rude and dismissive every time I'd attempted to interact with her and that she'd been away from the shop more than she'd been in it when I'd walked by—but I needed her help, and trashing her to her boss in front of her face wasn't going to do much to earn that. So instead I lied. "Oh, yes! She's been very helpful."

He looked faintly surprised, which made me wonder if my complaint wouldn't have been the first he'd ever heard about Sophie. Although if that was the case, I didn't know why he kept her on.

"In fact, I was coming by to thank her—she was so helpful when I came in yesterday. I really appreciated it." I met her eyes as I looked at her and smiled. For once, she had an expression that I wouldn't describe as loathful condescension. She actually looked surprised and maybe even a little grateful. I guessed my decision to be a bit of a brownnoser helped.

"That is wonderful!" Jacques patted Sophie on the back. "What did you get? Did you like it?"

"Macarons. They were—" I paused to think of the best word. "Divine."

Jacques beamed. "They are my specialty, you know."

"I know!" And then the dam burst, and words just spilled out. "I'm—I'm such a fan of yours. I got the last copy of your cookbook over in the gift shop, and I can't wait to try the recipes out. I own a coffee shop down at the beach, and I do all the baking for it— nothing like what you do, of course. I mean, I could never come close to these things." I waved my hands at the pastry cases around the shop. "But that just means I know how much work it is and how talented you are, and oh—" I clapped my hand over my mouth. It was the only way I could stop myself from babbling and embarrassing myself any more. "I'm so sorry."

"No, no! It's fine. It's wonderful to hear that someone enjoys my baking so much!" He gave me a warm smile that made me almost as happy as his macarons had. "You know me. I am Jacques. But what is your name, *cherie*?"

"Fran. Francesca."

"Francesca. Beautiful name! Tell me, are you staying here in the hotel, Francesca?"

"Yes." My babbling had apparently been replaced by monosyllables. Not exactly the impression I wanted to make on one of my baking heroes.

"Wonderful! It's a beautiful hotel, *non?*"

"Very beautiful."

"And many good restaurants inside! Did you know that all the desserts in those restaurants are from my kitchen here?"

My mind blanked, and I couldn't remember if that was something I knew before that moment or not. So I said no.

"They do. I make them all myself! Would you like to see where they come from?"

It took me a second to fully process that he was asking me if I wanted to see his kitchen—the kitchen where the great Jacques de Gaulle baked, day in and day out. "Yes!" I blurted it out a little too loudly and excitedly, but fortunately Jacques just smiled.

"Then, please, come with me." He walked to the swinging door to the kitchen and pushed it open. I walked through into a stainless steel and marble wonderland, covered with bowls of chocolate, trays of drying macarons, and carts of plastic-wrapped delicate pastries ready to be taken to the restaurants where they would be served. I stared at it in awe and fought back a nearly undeniable urge to taste everything in the place. I didn't think Jacques would appreciate that though, so I stood stock-still and looked around at everything.

"Francesca, I will be right with you. Feel free to look around." He let the door close partway but held it open as he paused to talk to Sophie. They spoke in French, so I didn't understand most of it, but I didn't need to understand a language to hear spite in someone's voice. And if I wasn't mistaken, that spite was directed at the person whose name was the one word I was pretty sure I did understand. Garrett.

Chapter 12

I DON'T KNOW how long I spent in the Pâtisserie Alford kitchen, but it was longer than I'd ever dreamed. Jacques showed me everything. He even gave me a few tips for getting my macarons to turn out just right. By the time he let me go with a promise to bring my copy of his cookbook down for him to sign, I was bubbling over with excitement and itching to spend some time in the kitchen baking. Of course, that would have to wait since it was only Saturday, and Matt and I weren't due to check out of the hotel until Monday. And I had a murder to solve.

Jacques kissed me on each cheek as I left, and I practically floated back out into the front of the bakery.

I crashed right back down to earth when I saw Sophie, still with her sour face. Although even I had to admit she looked slightly less like she'd been sucking on a lemon than usual. Only slightly though.

I sighed. She was the last person I felt like dealing with, but she was actually where she was supposed to be for once, and she *had* seemed grateful to me for covering for her with Jacques. I needed to make my move before her goodwill had a chance to wear off.

I smiled at her. She pursed her lips in what wasn't quite the most irritated look I'd seen on her face.

"It must be great working here! All these delicious desserts. Do you love it?"

She looked at me blankly, as though she hadn't heard me or wasn't quite sure that I was talking to her. Finally, she must have decided that I wasn't going to go away until she answered me. "It is fine."

"Really? It's just fine? I would love to work for someone like Jacques de Gaulle!"

Her slim shoulder twitched in what seemed to me like a very French shrug.

I walked over closer to her and leaned on the counter like she had actually been participating in the conversation with me. "Did I hear you and Jacques say something about Garrett right before I went in the back? He's the hotel manager, isn't he?" I was hoping that if I sounded friendly and conversational, she'd open up to me. I had no such luck.

"*Oui*" was all I got out of her.

"I heard him talking to Whitney at the front desk

yesterday, and he was pretty nasty to her. Is he always like that?"

Nothing.

Might as well go the obvious route. "Isn't he the one Amber thought killed Gina?"

"I have work to do. You should go." She didn't even try to make it look like she had something else to do. She just stood behind the counter and stared off into space instead of at me.

At that point, I gave up the hope of ever getting anything out of her. She was either just rude, or she hated me for some reason.

I looked over at her as she continued staring off into space. It couldn't be a French thing—Jacques had been overwhelmingly warm and friendly. I had to assume it was just a Sophie thing.

"Okay, well, good luck getting your work done," I said cheerfully even though I knew she wouldn't have cared if I'd just walked out. Just in case her issue was a two-day-long bad mood or something equally improbable, I wanted her to think I was a nice person. "I know I'll be back to get some more yummy desserts to try, so I'll see you later!"

She took a moment out of her staring to scowl at me.

I gave her a big smile back, like her behavior was totally normal, and walked out of the patisserie to figure out what I should do next.

Before I had time to think about anything though,

my cell phone rang. I fished it out of my pocket and realized it was Matt. The time also showed up on the screen, and I cringed as I realized how long I'd been gone. No wonder he'd woken up and was looking for me.

"Hey!" I said cheerfully, like there was nothing at all unusual about me wandering around a hotel all by myself when I was supposed to be having some quality time with my loving boyfriend.

"Where are you?" He actually sounded like he'd just woken up.

"I'm downstairs. Did you just wake up?" I wandered a few feet across the hall and leaned against the wall. I realized after just a second that I could still see Sophie inside the bakery, but unless she craned her neck, she probably wouldn't notice me where I stood. This seemed like an opportunity. I scooted a little bit farther down the hall just to make sure I was out of sight and settled in to watch her.

"Yeah," Matt croaked. "What are you doing downstairs?"

"Oh, nothing, just—" I stopped as Sophie walked around the counter and toward the front of the shop. I took a couple of steps back to try to keep out of sight. "I, um, just—" I ducked behind a bump in the wall as she walked out into the hallway. I didn't have to worry though—she didn't so much as glance my way, just turned and headed for the lobby.

"You're working on that murder investigation for Mike, aren't you?"

"Umm—" I kept my eyes on Sophie as I started following her down the hall. I tried to keep my footsteps quiet and stayed close to the wall in case she happened to turn around. "What did you say again?"

"You're working on the murder investigation, aren't you?" he repeated.

"Yes."

Sophie stopped, and I ducked behind a large potted plant.

Matt yawned on the other side of the phone. "Will you be done soon? I'm hungry."

Sophie resumed her walk, glancing into the lobby lounge as she passed by.

"Um, yeah. I'm just following—" I stopped myself. Matt probably didn't want to hear that I was trailing Sophie on her way to… wherever she was going. It could have been the bathroom, for all I knew, but I doubted it. There was a much closer one the other way. "I'm just following up on something."

"A'right." Matt groaned like he was stretching. "I'm going to get a quick shower, and then I'll be ready to go get something to eat. Do you think you can be back up here in like twenty minutes?"

Knowing Matt, it would take him at least fifteen minutes to drag himself out of bed and into the shower. I had a good half an hour before I needed to be back upstairs. "Yeah, that should be fine."

We said goodbye, and I slid my phone back into my pocket.

Past the lobby, Sophie slowed down, and so did I. As she put her hands on her hips and started turning around, I slipped into a doorway to hide. I could barely see her from my vantage point, and I knew she was there, so I hoped she wouldn't notice me. She crossed her arms and managed to look even more impatient and annoyed than usual.

She finally heaved a sigh, spun on her heel, and disappeared through a door across the hall from where I was still trying to make myself as inconspicuous as possible. I glanced down the hall to see if anyone was coming before I followed her. A figure was just disappearing through another door on the other side of the lobby. I realized at that moment that she must have been waiting for whoever it was. I could have kicked myself for not thinking to look that way sooner so I could have seen who it was. But that metaphorical ship had sailed, and no one else was in the hallway, so I hurried across to see where Sophie had gone through the door.

It opened out into the courtyard, but Sophie was gone. I had missed my chance.

I was so annoyed with myself as I headed back the other way. I briefly considered wandering out into the courtyard, just in case I could spot her, but even if I did, I doubted I would be able to find her without her seeing me. And as soon as she saw me, it was all over.

Whatever she was sneaking off to do, she would abandon, and I'd be back to square one. I was better off going back up to the room to freshen up before Matt and I went to eat.

Just before the lobby, I stopped in my tracks. I'd thought that Sophie's attitude came from either her innate rudeness or some mystical hatred she had of me, but now I realized there could be a third possibility—maybe she had something to hide.

I'd followed her from the patisserie out of curiosity—I just wanted to know where she disappeared to whenever she was conspicuously not at the counter. But what if she had another reason to be gone? I couldn't help but think I wouldn't mind if I found out that Sophie was the one who had killed Gina.

I needed to talk to someone who knew more about the inner workings and interpersonal politics of the hotel. Someone who would know who was acting weird and who was always rude and grouchy. Someone who I could actually get to share the inside scoop. Fortunately, I knew exactly who to talk to.

Chapter 13

I MADE a beeline for the front desk. Whitney had proven more than willing to talk to me when I met up with the girls outside. I had little doubt that she'd be happy to share more with me if I just asked the questions.

The desk was empty. I heaved a sigh of disappointment. Where had she gone? I could have sworn she was there when I passed through a few minutes before while I followed Sophie.

I drummed my fingers on the front desk as I tried to figure out what to do next. I still had at least twenty minutes before I had to be back upstairs.

"Can I help you?"

I jumped and spun around at the loud man's voice behind me. It was Garrett.

"Oh! No, I—uh—just—um—" I stammered, trying to think of a good reason I was at the desk, other than "covertly working on a murder investigation." For one thing, I didn't know if Garrett was involved, and for another, I didn't like or trust him.

Fortunately, Garrett's abrasive personality wasn't interested in waiting to hear what I had to say. "Where is Whitney? She should be out here! I swear, it's impossible to find good help these days. But you must know that since you have your own business."

Funny, I didn't remember telling him that. Maybe I'd just forgotten, or maybe he had some other perfectly good reason to know. Or maybe he'd been nosing around. I wouldn't put it past him.

"What do you need? Towels? A toothbrush? We'll of course be happy to provide anything you may have forgotten. We also have laundry services if you need them."

"Towels," I said quickly. He was annoying, but at least he'd given me an excuse for being at the desk.

"Certainly. I'll have housekeeping bring some up."

"Oh, we're about to go eat."

"No matter." He gave me a smarmy smile. "They can use their key to drop them off inside when they refresh your room." He moved over to the computer and started clicking buttons. "I'll just put a note in here that the two of you need some extra towels."

The look he gave me made my skin crawl. From anyone else's mouth, "extra towels" would have sounded perfectly innocent, but somehow he made it sound gross.

"Thanks, that'll be great." I turned to make my escape. The sooner I was away from him, the better.

"Oh, Francesca!"

I turned back around slowly. I did not like the way he said my name.

"I'm very sorry about what you witnessed in the spa yesterday. I hope you didn't see anything too... untoward."

A chill went down my spine. Was he threatening me? Did he have a reason to be threatening me? I should have just thanked him and walked away, but that would have been too sensible. "How did you know we were down there?"

His thin lips curled up in what I assumed was supposed to pass for a smile. "I'm the hotel manager. It's my job to know these things. Enjoy your brunch, Francesca." He gave me one last leering look then went back to tapping on the computer. I took the opportunity to escape.

Just before I stepped out of the lobby, I glanced back at the front desk. Garrett's dark eyes were still staring at me. I hurried away down the hall, grateful to be out of his sight. At least, I was until I noticed all the cameras in the hallways. I hadn't seen them before, but I guessed that was the point. They were supposed to blend in so people didn't think about the fact that they were being watched all the time. They made sense for security, of course, and under other circumstances, I'd be glad that they were there, but now all I could think about was Garrett sitting in a darkened room somewhere, watching me move around the hotel. It gave me chills.

But then I realized something. If there were cameras in the hallways in the main part of the hotel, wouldn't there be cameras in the spa as well? At least in the common areas. I hoped there weren't any in the locker rooms or treatment rooms. I had to talk to Mike.

I almost stopped at his door before I realized that Sandra probably wouldn't appreciate me showing up, especially not to talk about murder. Instead, I continued down the hall to my room. I heard the shower running and popped my head in to let Matt know I was back. He was still standing at the sink with his toothbrush in his mouth.

"Hi! I'm back."

He gestured and made some noises that I took to mean he was just about to get into the shower.

"Okay! I'm just going to go sit on the balcony while I wait."

He gave me a thumbs up, and I crossed the room to the balcony.

I sank down into one of the chairs, propped my feet up, and took a minute to soak in the scenery. The weather was beautiful. It was cool but not cold. The leaves had finally returned to the trees and were the bright green of springtime. The hotel gardens were colorful and vibrant with tulips and daffodils, and beyond them, I could see the bright-green grass of the golf course. It was a perfect Western Massachusetts day.

I could have sat out there and stared at the mountains forever, but I had a murder to solve. I pulled out my phone and dialed Mike's number.

"You find me some evidence yet?" he asked instead of saying hello like a normal person.

I wasn't letting him get away with that. "Well, hi, Mike! I'm good, how are you?"

"I'm good, thanks. Do you have any evidence yet?" He was not amused.

I decided the battle wasn't worth fighting. "No, but I have an idea of where you could find some."

Sometimes I thought Mike didn't have any manners, but I'd seen him be charming with people before, so I knew that wasn't true. He just didn't seem to feel the need to exercise that charm with me.

"Do you want to know?"

He sighed. "Yes, Fran. Where can I find this evidence you think might exist?"

"The cameras. There are cameras all through the hallways. There must be some in the spa too. It should be easy to see who else went in the treatment room to kill Gina." I waited proudly for him to tell me what a genius I was.

"The cameras weren't working."

"What?" I sat bolt upright. "What do you mean they weren't working?"

"They stopped recording around noon yesterday and were offline until sometime after the police arrived."

"You're joking."

"I wish I were."

I sank back into the chair. "Did they say what happened?"

"Hotel manager claims that this happens sometimes, a glitch in the network or something."

Hotel manager. Garrett. "You sound like you don't believe him."

"I don't. And neither do the local police. But there's no way to prove he had anything to do with it."

I couldn't believe that. There had to be some indication of his involvement. "But there must be! Has anyone checked the footage from right before they went out? Maybe you can see him going into the control room and turning them off."

"They checked that. But apparently whoever tampered with them knew what they were doing. Or else there really was a network glitch."

"Right during the time period of the murder? Likely story," I muttered. It had to be the other option. Garrett—or whoever disabled the cameras—had to have been smart enough to delete the footage of them going into the camera control room. "Did anyone other than Garrett have access to the control room?" If they didn't, it seemed like a slam dunk against Garrett.

Mike groaned. "Who didn't? Actually, I can tell you that—anybody they managed to forget to point it out to. There were no access restrictions on the door at all. Anybody could have just walked in there anytime they wanted, probably even you if you wanted to. For a big hotel, they are surprisingly lacking in security."

That wasn't what I wanted to hear. Although, I supposed that if Garrett was the only one who had access, the police would have arrested him already. It was so frustrating, feeling like the evidence should be right there but finding out that it just wasn't. Of course, if it was easy, Mike wouldn't have asked for my help, and the police would have already made an arrest. Still, maybe the cameras weren't a totally lost cause. "Did all the cameras go out or just the ones in the spa?"

"They all went out for about five minutes, then everything except the spa came back online. Everything went back out a while later, and that time when they came back on, all the cameras were working again."

"So someone obviously turned them off and back on."

"That's what it looks like to me. But Garrett said that's what's been happening. The system glitches in and out, sometimes everything comes back. Sometimes it doesn't. He said the spa has the most issues."

"Sounds awfully convenient." The shower turned off, and I remembered that Mike was supposed to be spending time with Sandra, just like I was supposed to be spending time with Matt. "Where's Sandra?"

"She's in the shower. I can only talk for another couple of minutes before I have to go."

"That's okay," I said, sighing. "That was the only thing I wanted to tell you, and it wasn't very useful."

"Not your fault. It was a good idea." He was being uncharacteristically nice. And it sounded like he was chewing something, which may have had something to do with it.

"Matt and I are about to go to brunch, so I'll get back to work after that."

"Sandra and I are about to go down too." Apparently, he wasn't letting that stop him from snacking, because I could still hear chewing. "Wait, which restaurant are you going to?"

"I don't know yet. Why? Do you want to meet us there?" I was teasing. I knew it was the opposite.

"Something like that," he muttered through some more chewing. "By the way, Fran, these cookies you had me get for Sandra are great. Well, that rose one was weird, but the others have been good."

"Those were supposed to be for Sandra! How many have you eaten?"

"A couple," he said quietly.

I doubted he was telling the truth.

"We're going to go get more later on anyway. She got excited when I told her about all the different kinds. I have a feeling I'm going to have to hold her back from blowing all my money on them. Those things are expensive."

"Consider it an investment in your marriage."

He made a thoughtful grunting noise before saying, "I better go. Let me know when you find something else out."

My stomach rumbled as we said goodbye and hung up. Apparently, it had finally realized that we'd skipped breakfast. At least Matt sounded like he was almost done in the bathroom and we could go to brunch soon. And I needed a cup of coffee like nobody's business. I was tempted to slip down to the lobby and see if I could grab something from the coffee bar, but with the way things seemed to work around here, it would probably be empty, and then Matt would come out while I was gone and be annoyed that I was delaying brunch even more. And then I'd have no coffee and a grumpy boyfriend, which was worse than no coffee and a happy boyfriend. Somewhat. No coffee was pretty bad.

Luckily, Matt came out of the bathroom before I had the chance to make a bad decision.

"You ready?" he asked, rubbing a towel over his wet hair, making it stand on end. "What?"

I couldn't help but grin. "You look so cute with

your hair all—" I waved my hands around my head in a general representation of the unruliness of his hair.

He patted it down into an approximation of a style. It still looked pretty cute. "So can we go? I'm starving."

"We can go."

As we made our way downstairs and over to the restaurant that was supposed to have the most heavenly brunch options, I filled Matt in on what I'd been up to while he lounged in bed. He listened in silence but looked skeptical. He was usually busy at work while I ran around Cape Bay, trying to figure out who was responsible for whatever mayhem was currently being wreaked around town. He'd catch the highlights at the end of the day, but he didn't usually get the live play-by-play.

"Sounds like you had a busy morning," he said when I'd finished.

"I did. I just wish I had more to show for it."

Fortunately for him, we got to the restaurant before I could get into my plans for the afternoon. It was probably best that he didn't know. Not yet anyway.

I looked around the dining room as the host took us to our seats, checking to see if Mike and Sandra were anywhere around. Not that I particularly minded if they were there. It was more that Mike's eyes boring into me during the meal would be a little distracting. I didn't see them, so I happily settled in at the table, with my back to the door. If Mike came in and wanted to glare at me, he could have at it. I was going to have a tasty brunch.

And, let me tell you, that menu was nothing if not mouthwatering. Every single thing on it looked amazing, from the eggs benedict to the French toast to the buttermilk waffles to the vegan tofu scramble. Okay, maybe the vegan tofu scramble wasn't quite my style, but I was sure it would have been delicious, based on everything else on the menu.

Matt ordered the eggs benedict, which was basically eggs with egg sauce since the key ingredient in that yellow hollandaise sauce that made eggs on an English muffin into eggs benedict was egg yolks. That didn't make it any less tasty, of course. I might have gotten it and, in fact, considered it but decided on the waffles instead because it would have been weird to dump maple syrup on eggs benedict, and I really wanted to cover my breakfast in maple syrup. The menu boasted that their syrup came from a farm just down the road, and I just couldn't pass that up.

The food came out looking amazing. My soft, fluffy-looking waffles were topped with pillowy, fresh whipped cream and a locally made strawberry compote. I couldn't see much of Matt's eggs benedict because it was thoroughly coated in a thick, rich, creamy hollandaise. We dug in enthusiastically.

As we started to eat, I think we both realized that we were even hungrier than we had known. We both practically inhaled our meals. It helped that the food was absolutely amazing. For the most part, a waffle is a waffle is a waffle, but something about these ones were extra delicious, even before I poured the syrup on top. Of course, once I tasted the syrup, I didn't have another bite without it. It may actually have been good on eggs benedict, but I was still glad I got the waffles. They were perfect.

When I finally mopped up the last bit of syrup with the last bit of waffle, I was satisfied but sorry that it was gone. I wished I were hungry again so I could start the meal all over, but there was no way I could have eaten even one more bite.

We dragged ourselves away from the table and started the walk back across the hotel toward our room. We didn't have any real plans for the afternoon other than relaxing and spending time together. Besides investigating Gina's murder for Mike, of course. I hoped to work on that in between taking a long walk around the grounds with Matt and maybe taking a nap in that big, soft, comfortable bed.

The restaurant was on the opposite side of the hotel from our room, so we had to cross through the lobby to get there. Out of a growing habit, I looked at the desk as we passed and saw Whitney smile and give us a quick wave. My steps slowed ever so slightly. Matt looked back at me with a question in his eyes. I debated the situation quickly. On the one hand, I knew that I was at the hotel to be with Matt, but on the other hand, I'd promised Mike that I'd find out whatever I could about Gina's murder. Plus, I was really looking forward to our massage the next day, and I was afraid it might end up being cancelled if the police didn't get things wrapped up before then.

"Franny?" he asked, apparently getting tired of waiting for me to explain why I was creeping through the lobby at a snail's pace while staring absently off into space.

I pulled him over toward one of the large fluted columns supporting the ceiling that arched a good forty or more feet above us. "I need to go talk to Whitney over at the desk." I grabbed his shirt and pulled him back toward me as he turned to look at Whitney. I didn't think she noticed. "It won't take long. I promise. You can go hang out in the lounge while I talk to her for a minute."

He looked a little uncertain but nodded reluctantly and turned to head that way.

"Ooh, wait!" I grabbed his shirt again to pull him back to me. "If Tommy and Carrick are there, try to talk to them about the murder. Well, whoever's there, see if you can find out what they know!"

"I thought you were going to kiss me," he said, looking disappointed.

I smiled up at him. "If I kiss you, will you talk to them?"

He grinned back. "If I agree to talk to them, will you kiss me?"

I put my hands on either side of his neck, pulled his face down to mine, and kissed him softly. As I moved my lips away, he leaned into me, tipping his head to kiss me again. I ducked away. "Nope. We have investigating to do."

He shook his head slowly, his lips curling up in a smile. As he turned to walk away, I was pretty sure I heard him mutter, "The things I do for you."

I smiled to myself and went to talk to Whitney.

Chapter 14

WHITNEY SMILED BRIGHTLY as I approached the front desk. "Hi! How can I help you?" she chirped.

I considered coming up with a plausible lie about needing more towels or toilet paper and beating around the bush for a while until the murder (hopefully) came up naturally in conversation. I also considered just blurting out my questions—it certainly wouldn't have been the first time I'd used that approach.

Ultimately, I decided to go with the indirect-direct approach. "Have you heard anything about when the spa will reopen?"

She shook her head sadly. "I'm sorry, I haven't. You have a massage scheduled, don't you? When is it? Tomorrow?"

I nodded.

She grimaced. "Hopefully it'll be open again by

then. It's taking them a while to do the investigation, I guess."

"Have you heard anything about whether they have a suspect?"

She looked at me a little suspiciously, with one eyebrow raised ever so slightly. "I don't know." Then her eyes flicked back and forth, and she leaned toward me. "If Garrett catches me talking to you about this, I could get fired."

"So don't talk to me about that," I said casually. "Talk to me about Sophie."

"Sophie?"

I nodded. "Yeah, Sophie from the patisserie."

"Why do you want to talk about Sophie?" She looked even more suspicious now than she had before.

I shrugged like it was no big deal and had nothing to do with me trying to solve Gina's murder. "Just curious. She doesn't talk much, does she?"

The laugh that burst from her lips came so quickly that it was obviously genuine. "Sophie? God, no! Girl will hardly say boo to me, and we've known each other for like three years now. Don't take it personal. She does what she wants when she wants and how she wants."

"So, it's not unusual for her to be a little…" I trailed off, partly for effect and partly because I wasn't quite sure how to say what I wanted to say without, well, sounding like Sophie.

"Rude?" Whitney's tone made it clear that I had

nothing to worry about. "No, that's just Sophie. She is who she is, love her or hate her."

"And which way do you feel about her?"

She shrugged and shook her head with a half smile on her face. "It depends on the day. Some days she cracks me up and I love her, and others, I just… mmm." She shook her head again, this time with less of a smile. "She is who she is."

I wondered if that bad disposition fed into other bad behavior as well. But I didn't think it was time to ask that yet.

"Good to know she doesn't just hate me for some reason." I thought for a second, trying to come up with something else to ask other than whether she thought Sophie could be a murderer. "That reminds me, I've tried to stop by the patisserie a couple times, and no one was at the counter. Is someone else supposed to be working there too?"

Whitney looked surprised. "Really? No one's been there? Are you sure?"

I nodded. "We hung around for a few minutes one time to see if anyone came out, but no one did."

"That's weird." She made a face. "Jacques's a stickler about customer service. I don't think he'd be happy if he knew she wasn't there when she was supposed to be. You said it's happened more than once?"

"Yup. A couple times yesterday and this morning before I talked to you guys outside."

"Huh." She drummed her fingers on the desk. "I thought it was weird that she was out there this morning, but with Sophie, you never know. The door was unlocked and everything?"

I nodded. "Wide open."

"So weird." She stared off into space, with her lips turned down in a frown.

I gave her a minute before asking my next question. "Did Sophie and Gina get along?"

Whitney looked at me with an expression that could freeze lava. "Is that what this is all about?"

I rushed to smooth things over. "No! I was genuinely curious about Sophie. I own a café, and if one of my employees ever treated my customers like that—" I stopped, realizing I was talking about, if not her friend, then at least someone she was social with. "I'm sorry. I was just curious about the dynamics."

Whitney's expression relaxed slightly, though she still looked wary. "If you say so."

"What was Gina like?"

She looked like she was about to answer but then stopped. "Look, you seem like a nice lady and all, but if Garrett catches me talking to you about Gina, he'll fire me on the spot. I can't lose this job. It pays better than anything else around here, and I need the money for school. I'm sorry, but you should go."

I searched my brain for a way to salvage the situation. So far, Whitney was my best resource, and I couldn't lose her. But I couldn't pay her like the hotel could either. At least for now, I had to move on. "I understand. Thanks for talking to me. I'm glad to know Sophie doesn't just have some weird hatred of me."

Whitney chuckled a little. "Nah, that's just her. Don't take it personal. But if she gets too rude, come tell me, and I'll talk to her. I may not be able to get her to be nice, but at least she'll know she's not getting away with it."

"I will, thanks!"

I turned and headed for the lounge to see if Matt had been any luckier in his information gathering than I had been, if he'd even bothered to actually talk to them about it at all.

I peeked in and saw him apparently engaged in an animated conversation with Tommy. I knew it was probably about sports, but on the off chance they were actually talking about the murder, I decided to leave them alone. I walked back to the lobby to try to figure out what to do next. I could just sit down and poke around on my phone for a while, but that didn't seem like the most interesting or productive thing I could be doing.

"Looking for your boyfriend?" Whitney asked from the desk. "I think he's in the lounge."

"He is. He's talking to Tommy, and I didn't want to interrupt. I'm just trying to figure out what to do with myself for now."

"Have you been upstairs?"

"Yes?" I replied in confusion. She knew my room was upstairs, didn't she?

"Sorry, I mean in the original hotel." She laughed.

I shook my head slowly. I hadn't been, and I wasn't sure exactly what she meant anyway.

"Up on the second floor, we have a few of the old rooms open and decorated in the way they would have been back when the hotel first opened. On the far sides are the basic rooms that regular people would have stayed in, and in the middle is the Grand Suite. That's where the *really* rich people stayed. There are plaques up and stuff if you want to take a look. Oh, and we have a pamphlet somewhere." At almost the instant she ducked down under the desk to look for it, Garrett popped out of a doorway beside me. I breathed a sigh of relief that Whitney and I hadn't been discussing the murder. I could see why she was so nervous about it.

"Where is Whitney?" he bellowed immediately. He seemed to have a knack for appearing when she was looking for something, and I wondered if it was intentional on his part—if he watched her from somewhere and came out just to humiliate and scream at her. From what I knew of him so far, I wouldn't have put it past him.

"I'm right here!" She stood up, with the pamphlet in her hand, and passed it to me. "Here you go. This has more details about the rooms and their history and some of the furniture and stuff in there."

"And the artwork," Garrett said. "We have some fine pieces of art in the hotel that I'm sure someone like you would enjoy viewing." His head snapped toward Whitney. "Get her the brochure on the artwork."

She took a deep breath and pursed her lips. I could tell she was trying not to say something she would regret as she knelt back down behind the desk to look for the other pamphlet. If Garrett hated her being out of sight while she looked for things, I didn't know why he didn't just arrange for the brochures to be moved up on top of the desk. Probably because then he wouldn't have as much to yell at her about.

"I apologize for the poor service," he said, louder than he needed to, as he turned back to me. "Good help is *so* hard to find."

If I felt like he had already complained to me about that, it was because it hadn't even been two hours since he'd last mentioned it. I wanted to tell him that it might be easier if he tried being a little more pleasant, but I didn't really want to invite him to have a conversation about it, so I kept my mouth shut.

"Whitney has actually been wonderful. She's very helpful. And friendly," I said with a strained smile. As much as I wanted to ignore him, I wouldn't have felt right not standing up for her.

He raised his eyebrows and gave me a disdainful look. I was almost surprised he didn't tell Whitney to forget the art brochure since clearly I had no taste, but he mercifully didn't say a word for once.

Whitney stood back up with the brochure in her hand. "Here you go. It talks about all the different pieces and has a list of them by artist and location so you can find them easily." Her voice sounded pleasant enough, but after talking to her earlier, I could hear the strain in it now. The hotel must pay really well for her to put up with Garrett and all his nonsense.

"Thank you," I said as I took the pamphlet from her. I made a point to keep my voice as warm and pleasant as I could. I didn't know if it mattered to her, but I wanted to at least make an effort to let her know that someone appreciated her.

For a moment, the three of us stood there looking at each other. I didn't really want to leave until after Garrett did, just because I felt bad leaving Whitney alone with him. Unfortunately, he didn't look like he was going anywhere anytime soon, and I couldn't think of anything else I needed at the moment. I'd already asked for extra towels.

"Is there anything else we can do for you?" Garrett asked, pretty much sealing the deal on me having to walk away.

"Nope," I said reluctantly. I shot a sympathetic look at Whitney and turned to go before stopping because I actually did think of something. "Oh, Whit-ney," I said, looking pointedly at her instead of

Garrett. "If Matt comes out looking for me, could you tell him where I went?"

"Sure." She smiled, but I could tell it wasn't sincere.

"Great, thanks." I felt bad leaving her, but I didn't know what else to do. I cast one last look in her direction and headed for the old elevator.

Chapter 15

I TOOK a right as I stepped off the elevator on the second floor in the old part of the hotel. I'd taken that elevator once before, when Matt and I first arrived, but we'd gone straight to the third floor and over to our room. While the third floor had definitely had an early-nineteen-hundreds style, it was nothing compared to the second floor. This was like I had stepped straight back in time to an era when the wealthiest of the wealthy held week-long house parties for forty or so of their nearest and dearest, all of whom brought along their own servants because they couldn't possibly be expected to get dressed on their own.

Old portraits lined the walls, some of which had subjects who looked familiar and all of which had nameplates underneath with the name of the artist, the person in the picture, and the dates they'd stayed in the hotel. I recognized even more of the names than I had the faces. I didn't necessarily know what people like Enrico Caruso, J.D. Rockefeller, and J.P. Morgan were famous for, but I'd heard of them.

As I walked slowly down the hall, looking back and forth at the elegantly posed pictures, I wondered whether the hotel had commissioned the portraits during the people's stays or if they'd been acquired later. Either way, it seemed like a massive undertaking. I'd never had my portrait painted (and didn't know anyone who had), but I was pretty sure it was a lengthy process that involved sitting very still for a very long time. Did these people really have time for that when they were on their vacations? Maybe things were different for the very, very rich, especially the ones who lived a hundred years ago.

On the other hand, if the hotel had acquired the paintings later, that had to be a lot of work—and a lot of money—too. There was at least one portrait in every wall space between the room doors, sometimes two, and in at least one place, I saw four. That whole family was apparently famous and important—or maybe egotistical—enough that each one of them had their own portrait.

I finally got to the end of the hallway with the first period-styled room that I could look into. The floors in there, like the hallway, were thin-planked wood in a parquet pattern. *It must have taken an eternity for those to be installed*, I thought. And the price would have been astronomical. But of course, it was probably cheaper than the marble tile in the foyer, and it was the Gilded Age, after all, when the super rich had money to burn and a deep desire to show off their wealth to all their equally rich friends.

Inside the room, the walls were covered with wallpaper in a simple floral pattern. The bed was a single with a plain blanket. The only other furniture was a dresser and a stand with a washbasin and pitcher. When Whitney said it was basic, she wasn't kidding.

The room across the hall was also open and looked basically the same except for a different floral pattern on the wallpaper and a blanket on the bed that veered more blue than cream.

As I started back down the hallway to the next open room, I remembered the pamphlets Whitney had given me. Maybe they had something about where all the portraits had come from. I flipped through them as I made my way slowly down the hall. There was no one nearby, so I took my time, flipping the pages and keeping my eyes more on the brochure than on the doors around me. There was a whole page in the art brochure dedicated to the hallway. I stopped and leaned against the wall—in a rare spot where the deep-red wallpaper wasn't covered by a portrait—to read it.

I was barely two sentences into the pamphlet when I heard quiet voices nearby. I glanced up and down the hallway, but I was alone. *Probably someone in their room*, I told myself. Most of the rooms on the hall still functioned as active guest rooms, not show pieces. I went back to reading but quickly realized that the voices weren't hushed because they were behind a door but because their owners were whispering.

I looked around again, more carefully this time, and realized the door I'd stopped beside was cracked open. If I'd been standing even on the other side of the hallway, I wouldn't have been able to hear them.

"Are you sure they don't know?" one voice said quietly. It sounded like a female voice, but I couldn't hear well enough to tell if it was one I recognized. Of course, there were lots of women in the hotel, so it wasn't really likely that I would recognize the voice.

"They have no idea," said a second voice. This one was lower, definitely male. "Trust me, they're clueless." He chuckled quietly.

"Stop laughing!" the female voice said. "It's not funny!"

I didn't want to eavesdrop, so I turned to walk farther down the hall, but then the female voice said something that stopped me in my tracks.

"Our lives will be over if they find out it was us!"

There were obviously a lot of things that could refer to, but one stood out to me—murder.

"They're not going to find out," the male voice said confidently.

I leaned back against the wall in a spot where I didn't think they would be able to see me from inside the room. If it sounded like they were coming out, I would just book it down the hallway and hope they didn't think I'd been listening.

"But they might. They're investigating. They're looking at evidence. They're going to figure out it was us! That's how these things work. Don't you ever watch cop shows on TV?"

The man in the room chuckled. "Baby, it's not like we're being investigated by the NYPD. They're not going to figure it out. We'll be fine. Trust me."

"I wish I could. Maybe we should just turn ourselves in." I couldn't hear her well, but her voice sounded choked, like she was crying.

"Baby, no." His voice was even lower now, and I had to strain to hear what he was saying. "We just need to be careful for a few days. The heat'll die down soon, and everything will be back to normal."

She murmured something in response that I couldn't quite make out.

"Yes, I promise," he said.

Their voices fell silent or at least too quiet for me to hear. I crept a couple steps closer. I needed to be able to hear better. I needed to be able to identify the voices. I was obviously going to tell Mike about what I'd heard, but it wouldn't do much good if I couldn't tell him who I'd overheard.

"I need to get back before they notice I'm gone."

I nearly jumped out of my skin. The man's voice was louder and, if I wasn't wrong, closer. I had to get out of there and fast. I wanted to see who they were, but it wasn't worth the risk. If they so much as suspected I'd overheard them, I could be their next victim. I ran as silently as I could down the hall to the elevator. The hardwood floors were gorgeous, but I would have given anything for some nice plush carpet right then.

I punched the elevator button a couple of times, first the down button, then up, too, just in case that made it come faster.

I glanced back down the hall. They hadn't come out of the room yet, but I was afraid they would any minute.

I hit both buttons again, more than once. I could hear the ancient elevator's gears and cables groaning and prayed that the old, slow elevator would miraculously speed up.

I checked once more to make sure the coast was still clear then looked over the opposite way. I knew there was another elevator down there, but would it be any faster? Or at this point, should I just take the stairs? They were a long way down the hall, but maybe I could make it.

I heard a feminine laugh and looked again in the direction I'd come from. An elbow was poking out of the doorframe, and I knew it would be followed by a body with a head and eyes any second. I didn't have any more time to wait for the elevator or to run for the stairs. I looked around one more time and saw an open door nearby. I didn't know if it was someone's room, and I didn't care. All that mattered was that it would get me out of the hallway.

I turned and darted through the open doorway. I swung myself around behind the door and prayed that they hadn't seen me.

Chapter 16

MY HEARTBEAT POUNDED in my ears, making it hard to hear, but there were definitely footsteps approaching. I heard a murmur of voices, too, but I couldn't hear what they were saying, either because of the rapid throbbing of my heart or because they were trying to keep their voices down.

The footsteps got louder as I tried to slow my breathing and my heart rate. I peeked through the crack between the door and the doorframe but then pulled back, afraid they'd see my eyeball staring at them. That's all I needed—to be on the verge of escape and get caught because of my unbearable nosiness.

"Don't worry, babe. We'll be fine. They have no idea it was us."

The man's voice sounded like it was right outside.

I held as still as possible, tried not to breathe, and hoped it was enough.

The footsteps stopped.

"Stairs or elevator?" the man asked.

"Stairs. Less likely to get caught."

Now that they weren't whispering, I thought the woman's voice may have sounded familiar. Maybe his too. I couldn't be sure though, and I definitely didn't know who either of the voices belonged to.

The footsteps resumed, and I decided to risk peeking through the crack again. All I could see was their backs as they walked down the hall away from me. He was tall and thin, with dark hair, a black shirt, and fitted black pants. She was a good bit shorter, with long blond hair that hung in loose curls down her back. She was dressed head to toe in pale blue that looked like hospital scrubs.

I leaned back against the wall to process every-thing I'd heard and seen but was immediately distracted as I actually looked for the first time at the room I was in.

It was another of the show rooms, but this one wasn't remotely like the simple ones I'd seen down the hall. This one looked like something I'd see in a palace.

The floor was still the same wood parquet, but here the majority of it was covered by a massive, sumptuous Oriental-style rug that had to be an inch thick. The pattern on the wallpaper was fairly simple, but by the way it sparkled, I was pretty sure it was run through with actual strands of gold to accent the buttery-yellow base color. The bed wasn't the simple iron single of the other rooms. No, this one was a big four-poster with a canopy in a rich red that looked like velvet from where I stood. It looked like it was just a double, but it still looked elegant. The room was scattered with furniture—a table, a few chairs, a chaise, a desk, a bureau. The chairs and chaise were upholstered in the same rich fabric as the canopy. It looked like a room fit for a king.

I went to grab the brochures Whitney had given me out of my pocket but realized they were still clutched in my hand. And pretty wrinkled at that point too. I smoothed out the one about the display rooms and found the pictures of the room I was standing in. Apparently, it had belonged to the original owner of the hotel. His wife's room was down the hall, also available for viewing. From the picture, her room looked equally refined but blue instead of red.

I turned to go see it when I remembered why I was hiding in the owner's room in the first place. I had found the murderers. I didn't know who they were, but I had found them. I needed to tell Mike. But surely there wouldn't be a problem with going to look at one more room first, would there? I didn't see why there would be. It wasn't like I'd heard them planning a second murder. They'd been saying they were going to lay low. Taking five minutes to go look at the other room wouldn't hurt anything.

So that's what I did. I made my way down the hall to the room that had belonged to the lady of the house, back when it was a really fancy, elegant house and not a fancy, elegant hotel. And presumably not the site of a murder.

The room was every bit as elegant as the husband's, maybe even a little bit more. It was decorated in shades of blue instead of reds, and the furniture was a bit more delicate, with fluting and scrolls and dainty flowers carved into the wood. While the paintings on the wall in the other room had been mostly wild animals with a few ancient Greek classics thrown in, all the ones in here—and there were quite a few—were of flowers and gardens with a few bowls of fruit thrown in for good measure. Better yet, when I read the couple of paragraphs about the room in the pamphlet, it casually mentioned that among the paintings were two by Monet and Renoir, as though that were a totally normal thing to just have hanging around.

I tried for a moment to imagine myself living in that room, sleeping in that bed, lounging in that chaise. I tried to think of what it must have been like to sit at the vanity while a maid styled my hair, not for some fabulous event but just to go down to breakfast.

And what it would be like to need someone to help me dress, again, not in an evening gown with a zipper I couldn't reach, but just in an everyday dress, something that I would wear to take a walk in my expansive gardens.

I couldn't do it. It was altogether too ridiculous. I couldn't imagine being that helpless. Then again, the woman who had lived in this room probably couldn't have imagined prowling around, listening at doors, trying to solve a murder, so I guessed we all had our own strengths.

At that point, I realized I probably needed to get back downstairs. Aside from the fact that Matt was probably waiting for me and wondering where I'd wandered off to this time, I had a murder to solve. I even had suspects now. They were still unfortunately nameless, but they were suspects all the same.

I cast one last look around the room and headed for the elevator. I fully expected Matt to be standing in front of the elevator doors when they opened again, but the lobby was empty. I looked around for a second just to be sure then decided to go check the lounge.

Sure enough, there he was, sitting at the bar but turned toward where Carrick was standing, by the espresso machine, the two of them cracking up about something. Somehow I didn't think it was Gina's murder. At least I hoped it wasn't anyway.

I hovered in the wide arched opening between the

lobby and the lounge for a minute, wondering if I should go over and interrupt or just let them be. I'd already sucked so much fun out of Matt's vacation with the whole murder investigation thing that I thought maybe I should just let him enjoy himself for a little longer. Of course, he was supposed to be spending a romantic weekend with *me*, so maybe going over there was the better option.

The decision was taken out of my hands when Tommy came out from the swinging door behind the bar, spotted me, and waved in my direction.

Matt turned around and raised his glass in my direction. "Hey, Franny! Come on over."

I smiled awkwardly at the few people scattered around as I crossed over to the bar. "Hey, guys."

Matt slid his arm around my waist and pulled me close to him. "How'd it go, Franny? Find out what you wanted to know?"

I tried to keep myself from going bug-eyed. I pressed my nails into the back of his shoulder. What was he thinking? Other people weren't supposed to know what I was up to. If they did, the whole investigation could be compromised. But if I let on that I didn't appreciate him saying that, it could be even more of a tip-off to Tommy and Carrick that I was trying to find out who killed Gina.

So, I tried to sound as calm and casual as I could and hoped that Matt would catch on. "Yep! Whitney gave me some pamphlets about the art in the hotel and some of the historic rooms." I smiled at him with a little more intensity in my eyes than usual. "I even went ahead and snuck up to look at the rooms for a minute since I didn't think you'd be very interested."

Matt chuckled. "Good call."

"So what have you guys been chatting about? You sounded like you were having a good time when I walked up."

A look seemed to pass between the three of them that I didn't know the meaning of. Were they talking about the murder? About women? The relative merits of different kinds of whiskey? Or maybe what kind of season the Celtics were having? Knowing Matt, it was probably that, even though it wasn't what I'd sent him in there for.

"The Sox. These guys are big baseball fans." Matt nodded approvingly at the two of them. "Carrick played college ball, and Tommy had pro scouts coming to watch him pitch back in high school."

"I blew my arm out senior year. Never could throw a curve the same way again." He shook his head sadly.

I tried to look sympathetic even though I barely understood what any of that meant. Sports weren't really my thing.

They went on for a couple more minutes, talking about guys they'd played with who made it or almost made it. I listened politely but was relieved when Matt finally slugged back the last of his drink and stood up. "Well, boys, I better get going. As much as I've enjoyed this, I didn't come here to hang out with you guys."

"Charge it to the room?" Tommy asked.

"Yup."

Tommy pushed a slip of paper across the bar to Matt.

"I gotta say, I love this 'charge it to the room' thing," he said as he scribbled his name.

"You might not love it when you see the bill at checkout," I said quietly.

He winked at me and slid the receipt back to Tommy. "See you guys later." He put his arm around me and started guiding me across the lounge.

I was disappointed and maybe even a little frustrated that I had asked him to find out what Tommy and Carrick knew about the murder and he'd apparently spent the whole time talking about sports instead. I knew that probably wasn't fair in light of the fact that I'd basically co-opted the romantic getaway he'd planned and turned it into a murder mystery weekend instead, but it was how I felt.

As we turned to go down the hall toward the elevator up to our room, Matt pulled me closer to him. He tipped his head down, and for a second, I thought he was going to kiss me on the temple. But it was better than that.

"I see why you get caught up in these investigations," he whispered. "It's kind of fun."

I looked up at him, wondering if he meant what I thought—what I hoped—he did.

His eyes twinkled. "I found out some stuff I think you and Mike are going to be pretty interested in."

Chapter 17

MATT REFUSED to say another word about what he'd learned from Tommy and Carrick until we were alone in our room.

As soon as we walked in, it was obvious that housekeeping had been in while we were gone. The curtains were wide open, letting the bright spring sunshine pour in. The bed was neatly made with all the pillows fluffed and arranged perfectly.

The bathroom sparkled. The few cosmetics I'd left out had been moved to the side and arranged neatly. The towels we'd used were gone, and in their place was a massive pile of fresh ones. Apparently, Garrett had passed along my unnecessary request for more towels, and housekeeping had complied enthusiastically. I didn't think we could have used that many towels if we'd stayed for a week.

Something else had been dropped off while we

were gone too—a huge box of macarons. On top was a notecard with the hotel's logo. A smile spread across my face as I read it.

Mlle Francesca,

Merci beaucoup for letting me show you my kitchen today. It was an honor to share my passion with you. Please enjoy these macarons as a token of my appreciation!

P.S. Don't forget to bring the cookbook so I can sign!

It was signed, of course, Jacques de Gaulle. I tried not to swoon. Not only had *the* Jacques de Gaulle handwritten me a note and sent me a truly massive box of his macarons, but he had also *thanked* me—me! —for coming in to see his kitchen. I wondered for a second if I'd somehow accidentally led him to believe I was more important than I was, but no, I was pretty sure I had been clear that baking was something I did on the side and that I was just a fan of him and his work. He was just that lovely and charming.

I opened the box and took a moment to look at the rainbow assortment then grabbed a yellow-and-pale-pink lemon-lychee one. It was divine.

"Where did that come from?" Matt asked when he saw it.

"Jacques de Gaulle," I murmured, letting the tart citrus flavor roll around my tongue as I lay back on the couch. I held up the note for Matt to read.

"Wow. Looks like you made a good impression."

"I can be very impressive."

The corners of his eyes crinkled. "I know."

He sat down and grabbed a brown chocolate-hazelnut cookie. "So you want to hear what I found out?"

"I've already heard enough about their baseball careers," I grumbled. Matt had missed out on a prime opportunity to get information about the case. Not that he'd asked to be involved in the first place, but still.

"You were gone a long time. We had time to talk about other things too."

"You did? Like what?"

He gave me a sly look out of the corner of his eye. "Like murder." Matt popped the rest of his macaron in his mouth and reached for another, a pink-and-white strawberries and cream. Apparently, his experience wasn't as rapturous as mine, but then he didn't tend to feel that way about food.

I sat straight up. "Yes!"

"So, apparently it's like a soap opera around here."

I raised my eyebrows as I savored another bite of my lemon-lychee macaron.

"Everybody's sleeping with everybody. Everybody's bickering with someone. Tommy said he can't keep straight who hates whom on any given week." He shrugged. "Apparently, that's just how it is in restaurants and resorts like this. He said there's management, who tends to more or less stay out of it, and then there are the rest of the staff, who basically act like they're at summer camp." He looked thoughtful for a second. "Which I guess they kind of are."

It made sense. A bunch of young adults spending long hours working in close proximity were bound to have some drama. That was the premise of half the reality shows on TV.

Matt chuckled as he reached for yet another macaron. I resisted the urge to slap his hand away and tell him that they were mine and they were for savoring.

"Apparently, they've had an issue lately where someone's been sneaking into the unoccupied guest rooms and... well, you know."

"Really? Shouldn't they get in trouble for that?" I shouldn't have been surprised, especially given what he'd just told me, but I was. At least they were using unoccupied rooms though.

"Big trouble. The hotel manager is supposedly furious. Says he'll fire them on the spot and blackball them from any of the other hotels in the area. It's a big deal with the staff. The guy's been checking all the camera footage and the keycard logs, but whoever it is has some sneaky way to avoid all that stuff. Apparently, he's been threatening lately to have DNA tests done on everyone to match up with... you know."

"Oh wow! And ew! But wow. That's crazy." My chewing slowed as I started to put something together in my head. "Oh... oh... oh no."

"What?"

"I just realized—" I told him about what I'd seen upstairs and the couple I'd been eavesdropping on. "I was sure they were talking about getting away with Gina's murder, but now I realize they were probably just talking about not getting caught sneaking into the empty rooms."

Matt thought about it for a second then nodded. "Yeah, you're probably right."

"That's so disappointing. Now I don't have anything to tell Mike."

"Well…" He tilted his head and made a face Robert De Niro would have been proud of.

"What?"

"It's not much, but I did get a little bit out of them about the murder."

"Really? What?" I didn't know if it was the sugar from the cookie or excitement, but my hands were shaking.

"So we were just talking. They were telling me about all the drama behind the scenes and all, and Tommy's the one who said it's like a soap opera. Well, somebody's always dying on soap operas, right?" It was a genuine question, like he thought I watched a lot of soap operas or something.

I didn't really have time for them, but my grandmother had made sure she did, especially as she got older and my mom started taking over in the café. I'd caught more than a few episodes by angling my seat at the kitchen table so I could keep up with the latest goings-on in Port Genoa while I was supposed to be doing my homework. "Dying or fake dying."

He looked confused, but I waved my hand. It was too much to explain when I wanted to hear what he'd found out about Gina.

"Anyway, we were kind of joking around about the soap opera thing and all the drama between the employees, and I asked them if Gina was the kind of girl who was always in the middle of all that." He stopped like that was the end of the story.

"And?"

"Well, that's what was weird—one of the things that was weird. Carrick said no—she was a nice girl, kept to herself, didn't get involved in everything—but Tommy basically called her one of the instigators of everything. Said she was always in people's business. She acted all sweet and innocent, but she was a troublemaker."

"So one of them is lying." The trouble would be figuring out which one. Although, having met both Tommy and Carrick, I was inclined to believe Tommy.

"Well…" Matt managed to say a lot with just the way he drew out the one-syllable word.

"Well what?"

"Well, apparently Carrick hasn't been here that long. Tommy said he just hadn't had the chance to see the real Gina yet."

"That's not very helpful."

"Yeah, I know." He reached for another macaron. I would have stopped him, but I wanted to see what he thought of a lavender-sage combination.

Not much, apparently. His lip curled as soon as he tasted it, but the bite of cookie was already in his mouth. He looked around unsuccessfully for a napkin.

"You know, if you'd just swallowed it, it would have been out of your mouth already." I was amused but didn't want him to suffer. I also didn't want him to throw away the rest of the macaron. It definitely sounded like a weird flavor combination, but I wanted to try it, especially after seeing his reaction.

He cringed but swallowed. "It tastes like dusty soap!"

I held my hand out.

He shook his head. "No, you don't want it."

"Yes, I do. Let me try."

He made a couple more efforts to warn me off but finally gave in. I took a bite and had to admit he wasn't wrong. Still, I swallowed it down. I put the last bite on the table next to the box full of hopefully tastier macarons and shook my head. "Somebody must like it."

"I warned you," he muttered.

"Yeah, I know." I picked up a pistachio macaron to hopefully get the flavor of soap out of my mouth. Thankfully, it was much tastier. "So, what do you think? Is one of them lying, or did Carrick just not know Gina well enough yet?"

"They pay me to get information, not make decisions."

I shook my head. I might have to get Matt to tell Mike directly what he'd learned. Mike would probably have some insightful cop question that would make it obvious who was telling the truth. "Did you find out anything else? Other than what sports they played in high school, I mean."

Matt chuckled. "We talked about the hotel manager. Garner?"

"Garrett."

"Yeah. He seems like a jerk, just from what the two of them said."

"About the issue with someone using the rooms?"

He nodded, stretched, and put his feet up on the coffee table next to the box of macarons. I slid them away. Foot seemed like an even worse flavor than lavender-sage.

"He's my prime suspect."

"Oh yeah? Tommy agrees with you?"

"They said he asked her out a while back, and she said no. I guess he's not the kind of guy who responds well to that."

"Sounds like an understatement."

I decided that if Matt was getting comfortable, I should too and leaned back into the couch. Instead of putting my feet on the coffee table though, I put them on Matt's lap and wiggled my toes.

He dutifully dug his thumbs in and started massaging them. "Aren't I supposed to be paying someone a lot of money to do this for you this weekend?"

"The spa's still closed. That's why we're trying to get this murder solved, so I can have a professional do this instead." I turned my foot so he could have a better angle.

"Anyway, Tommy said this Garrett guy has gotten aggressive before. Not toward people, but he's been known to slam things and kick things. Threw a chair across a room once."

"Wow." I subtly moved my feet so he could massage the other one. "It's a long way from that to murder though." He may have been my prime suspect, but Mike would continue not caring about that until I brought him some evidence. I may not have been a detective, but I was pretty sure chair throwing wouldn't cut it.

"That's what Carrick said."

So they disagreed again. Interesting. "What did Tommy say about that?"

"More or less the same thing. Carrick hasn't been there long enough to know what Garrett's really like."

I groaned, partly because what little evidence I'd managed to find all seemed to contradict itself and partly because Matt had hit a really good spot on my foot.

"Anyway, then Tommy had to go in the back to take care of something, and Carrick and I got to talking about baseball again, so that's all I found out."

Before I could say anything else, the room phone rang. Matt and I exchanged a look. I couldn't remember the last time I'd heard a hotel room phone ring. I was closest, so I hopped up to get it.

"Hello?"

"Hi. Is this Fran?" a cheery voice chirped on the other end.

"Yes, it is."

"Great! Hi, Fran, this is Whitney. I was just calling to let you know that the police have released the spa, and housekeeping has been in to get it all spick and span, and it's back open. As compensation for the inconvenience, we're giving you a free day pass to enjoy the pool and other amenities. You're welcome to head on down to use it today, or you can save it for a later day in your stay. Do you have any questions?"

Other than how many times she'd rattled that spiel off and how many more times she still had to, I didn't and told her.

"Great!" She paused for a second, and I thought that was it, but it wasn't. "Did you make it upstairs earlier?" Her voice was lower. Not quite a whisper but almost like she didn't want anyone to overhear.

"Yes, I did—why do you ask?"

"Just wanted to make sure you made it up there and saw everything okay."

And then it hit me that she wasn't talking about the rooms. "Yes, I did. It was very interesting. Thank you for pointing me in that direction."

"Oh, you're welcome. A lot of guests seem to think they're really cool, and you seem like the type to like old stuff, so I thought I'd suggest it."

Or maybe she really was talking about the rooms after all. I was so focused on looking for clues I was making them up out of nowhere. "I did like them. Thanks."

"Okay, cool. Just go down to the spa whenever you want to use your pass. Talk to you later."

"Who was that?" Matt asked as I put the phone back down on the receiver.

"Front desk. The spa's back open, and we get a free day pass to use the pool and stuff."

"Cool. That didn't work out so bad, did it?" He cringed when he saw the look I was giving him. "Well, I mean, not for Gina or anything."

I nodded and pulled out my phone to make a call. This was actually unbelievably great news. Yes, Gina's killer was on the loose, but Mike had put me on the case so that the spa would be opened as soon as possible so that he and Sandra could get their massage so that they could get their marriage back on track.

"Who're you calling?" Matt asked, leaning over

my shoulder, clearly feeling a little bad for his comment.

"Mike," I mouthed just as he answered.

"Hello?" His voice on the other end sounded gruff and strained.

"Hey! Did you get the call that the spa is back open? Your massage isn't scheduled for another hour, right? So you can still make it."

"Yeah, they called me." He sighed heavily. "Sandra says she won't go."

Chapter 18

"WHAT DO you mean she won't go?"

Matt looked up at the sharp tone in my voice, but I wasn't really paying attention to him. I was paying attention to Mike on the other end of the phone.

"She won't go," Mike said, sounding drained. "The spa's open, but the police haven't made an arrest yet. She said she won't be able to relax, knowing that the person giving her a massage could be a murderer."

I bit my tongue—literally—to keep from spitting out any one of the sharp retorts that was running through my mind at the moment. Her masseuse could be a murderer *anyway*. If she needed the person to be arrested, did she need them to be convicted too? That would require the massage to be put off for a while.

Besides, Gina worked in the spa—it wasn't like

someone was bumping off strangers down there. Her murderer was probably someone with a grudge of some sort, not someone who just stumbled into the first open room and killed the person inside it. I hoped not anyway. That would be a game changer. But in any case, it was a couples massage—she wouldn't be alone with anyone but Mike. Did she really think that her masseuse was going to kill her while someone else was in the room and Mike was two feet away?

Despite all of those less-than-kind thoughts, I didn't blame her for feeling uneasy. Someone had been murdered down there after all. I'd probably feel a little uneasy when we went for our own massages, too, but I'd had a knot in my back from leaning over baking sheets for weeks now, and I wasn't going to let a little anxiety get in the way of someone digging in and working that thing out.

The one thought that I couldn't dismiss was that Sandra was a smart woman and generally far more levelheaded than I ever was, not at all the type to freak out over every slight risk or threat of danger. She was married to a cop, for heaven's sake. She couldn't be. But it was because of her typical poise and composure that I was a little bit suspicious of her reasoning. I couldn't help but wonder if what she was really nervous about was the status of her relationship with Mike and whether she was ready to get back together with him or continue the separation. A couples massage would be a definite move in one of those directions.

Or she may have just been feeling anxious about the murder.

"So, what are you going to do?" I asked instead of saying any of that.

"I don't know." Mike's voice was low and rough. It was the closest to emotional I'd ever heard him. Well, except for maybe that time when he saved my life, but that time he didn't sound like he was going to burst into tears. This time, as out of character as it was, it seemed possible.

I felt terrible for him. I knew how desperately he wanted things to work out with Sandra. And it was that desperation that I heard in his voice now and that made me want to do something—anything—to help him. "Do you think it would help if I talked to her?"

"I think it would help if you found the murderer. Have you gotten any evidence yet?"

Despite my sympathy for him and his predicament, I bristled a little bit at his implication that this was my murder to solve. It hadn't been my idea to investigate. I was supposed to be enjoying a romantic weekend with my loving boyfriend. I wasn't a cop. And goodness knew Mike had told me enough times to stay out of police business. And now he was getting on my case about not solving it quickly enough? It grated. I wanted to say so, but I bit my tongue yet again. He was going through a lot, and if he was depending on me to solve the case, he was obviously at the end of his rope.

I opened my mouth to tell him about the couple I'd overheard in the hallway near the historic rooms but then closed it again. There was no way I could tell him that without also telling him that someone had been using the unoccupied rooms for romantic rendezvous. Well, I *could* forget to mention it, but it wouldn't do any good. He'd find out soon enough, and then I'd be right back where I started. No evidence and nothing to tell him. It wouldn't even do any good telling him about what Matt had learned from Tommy and Carrick. Everything either of them said contradicted what the other one said.

"No, nothing yet."

He heaved a sigh that oozed either deep disappointment or discouragement, maybe a combination of both.

"Now that the spa's back open, I think I'm going to go down there and try to see what I can find out," I blurted out, wanting to give him at least a little bit of hope. Until that moment, I'd had no such plan, but apparently, I did now. Judging by Matt's face, he was none too pleased about the sudden change in plans.

"Okay, good." Mike sounded instantly more cheerful but not much. It was Mike after all. "Let me know what you find out." He barely said goodbye before hanging up.

Matt's eyebrows were raised when I looked at him.

I sighed and told him about Sandra.

"And what does that have to do with you?"

"Mike was upset."

Still with his eyebrows up, still the skeptical look.

"I don't know. It just came out. I felt bad for him. I wanted to help."

Matt sighed and leaned back on the couch, rubbing his forehead. "I just wish we'd known ahead of time that you'd be into this. I could have gone golfing."

"Well, that wouldn't have been very romantic."

His eyebrows—which had returned to their normal position only moments before—shot back up. "And you running around investigating a murder is?"

"Good point." I tried to think of how I could fix the situation. "You could come down to the spa with me."

It didn't seem possible, but his thick, dark eyebrows went up even higher.

"What? You're the one who decided to take me on a mini spa vacation. I'm just trying to get us down to the spa together."

"I envisioned it more as lounging in a sauna than interrogating suspects," he said drily.

"I know. But Mike—"

"Mike better appreciate all the work you're doing on this," he grumbled.

"He does." I sighed. At least I thought he did. It was hard to tell with him sometimes.

Matt gave me a serious look. "Do you really think it's safe for you to go poking around down there? Somebody was murdered yesterday, you know."

"It'll be fine." I stood up and straightened my shirt, unsuccessfully trying to smooth out the wrinkles that had resulted from my hurried packing.

Matt looked doubtful. "Just be careful, okay?"

I smiled and bent down, resting my hands on his shoulders. "I promise I will." I went to brush a kiss across his lips, but he grabbed me and pulled me down onto the couch with him, making the kiss much more intense than I'd planned. I kissed him back for a few seconds before gently pushing him away. "I really need to get down there. Mike is counting on me."

I thought for a second that he was going to kiss me again. Instead Matt shook his head but had a smile on his face. "Blame Mike all you want. I know you do it because you're nosey."

I wanted to argue, but I couldn't. Well, not much. "I'm naturally curious."

He grinned and flicked the TV on. "Call it what you want. You can't stand a mystery. You hate not knowing what's going on."

He was right, of course, but I couldn't admit that, so I ignored it. I almost leaned over to kiss him again but knew it would just delay my mission even further. "I'll be back in a bit."

"Be careful."

"I will." I cast one last look over my shoulder at him as I headed for the door.

His only reply was a grunt. He was already glued to the basketball highlights on whichever sports network he had managed to land on first. More likely than not, he'd be asleep before I made it to the elevator, which was fine by me. It would give me more time to figure out who to talk to down in the spa, get ahold of them, and convince them to tell me something that would blow the case wide open.

Chapter 19

THE GIRL at the desk refused to let me in without an appointment or a spa pass. I could have gone ahead and used the day pass the hotel had offered me—the girl even asked about that—but I was pretty sure Matt would have appreciated that even less than he appreciated me running around investigating Gina's murder. That would have been a step too far.

So after unsuccessfully trying to get the receptionist to talk to me about Gina, I was reduced to wandering down the hall outside the spa, hoping to run into either a good idea or someone who would talk to me.

I wasn't optimistic. An employee would be my best bet, and they probably had back hallways to use when they came and went. They probably weren't just wandering the main hotel halls. And even if they were, I doubted they'd talk to me after Garrett had come down so hard on them and threatened their jobs. But I wasn't quite ready to give up, so I walked slowly back and forth, hoping that, by some stroke of luck, I'd run into someone who didn't know or care about Garrett's threat.

And then I did.

Amber was sauntering down the hallway in my direction when I spotted her. Her long chestnut hair cascaded over her shoulders. I wondered if she gave treatments with her hair like that. I tried to think of what it had looked like when I first saw her the day before, but all I could remember was the horror on her face as she stumbled, screaming, out of the room where she'd found Gina's body. I couldn't, for the life of me, remember how she'd worn her hair. Not that it mattered. I just had a serious case of hair envy, comparing her glossy curtain of hair with my unruly mop. That's not to say that I didn't appreciate my own thick waves, just that her hair was truly stunning. Maybe it was something in the hotel's water—almost everyone had gorgeous hair, no matter what the texture. Amber's hair was long, shiny, and straight. Whitney's kinky curls had a gorgeous sheen, and Sophie's sleek bob was utterly flawless. Even the blonde I'd seen upstairs had bouncy waves that looked like they were out of a magazine. Maybe I needed to soak my hair in the sink for a while. Or book an appointment with one of the stylists in the salon. That would probably be easier.

"Amber?"

She stopped and looked at me, clearly not able to place me at first, but recognition dawned on her face after just a few seconds. "You were outside earlier."

I nodded and held out my hand to shake hers. "I'm Fran."

"Amber," she murmured even though I obviously knew since I'd just called her that.

I hesitated. I wanted to talk to her about Gina, of course, but I wasn't sure if she would. Maybe if I could ease into it, but I didn't know what else to bring up to get her talking. I was going to have to think fast. "I'm sorry about your friend." Not the most original, and I was pretty sure I'd already said it to her, but it was the best I could do on very short notice.

"Thanks." She leaned against the wall and started examining her hair for split ends.

"She worked down here with you?"

She nodded and grabbed another section of hair.

"You two were close?"

Another nod. This wasn't very productive. But she wasn't telling me to shove off either.

I took a step closer to her so I could lower my voice to where it wouldn't be overheard. "You said you think Garrett did it?"

She flicked her eyes up at me for just a second, and I thought she was going to tell me to get lost, but she just went back to examining her hair. "I dunno.

He was a jerk, and he hated her. It would make sense."

She didn't sound nearly as confident about his involvement as she had that morning. It was the opposite of what I needed—doubt instead of evidence. But maybe she just needed a little prodding. "Did you see him down here?"

She shook her head. "Noelle banned him a while ago. He kept coming down, being loud, and bothering the clients."

"She has that kind of authority?"

She shrugged without looking up. "He stopped coming."

It was interesting, but I wasn't sure it was useful. "Did you see anyone else around who wasn't supposed to be there?"

She looked at me out of the corner of her eye without turning her head. "You some kind of Nancy Drew or something?"

I didn't know kids read Nancy Drew anymore. I had read maybe one or two of them growing up and gave up because they seemed hopelessly old fashioned. But I had Amber's attention, and I wasn't going to risk losing it because I got distracted by Nancy Drew, so I shrugged. "Just curious is all."

"Sure you are," she scoffed but didn't seem like she cared. She grabbed another section of hair and ran her finger across the ends, fanning them out.

"So did you see anyone?"

She flicked her eyes at me again then sighed and went back to examining her hair. "I wish I had," she muttered. "I keep thinking about it, trying to figure out if I missed anything. I mean, somebody went in there, right? Why didn't I see them?" She shrugged and brought her hair closer to her face.

Before I could say anything else, a familiar face walked out of the spa. "Sandra!"

She looked at me and smiled, or at least made an effort to. It had to be just about the saddest smile I'd ever seen.

"Fran. Mike said you and Matt were here."

I held my hand out to catch her arm. "Wait here a second. I want to talk to you."

She looked hesitant but stayed next to me while I turned back to Amber.

"Is there any way Garrett could have gotten into the treatment room without you seeing him?"

Amber didn't react at all.

"Amber."

She looked up at me disinterestedly. "Huh?"

I repeated my question, slower this time.

Her shoulder twitched in a shrug. "I mean, maybe without me seeing him, but somebody would have seen him there. We all know him. And he's not, like, the kind of guy you don't notice or something."

I hadn't been at the hotel long, but I could see her point. Garrett wasn't exactly shy about making his presence known, but even if he didn't announce himself, everyone knew him. People wouldn't forget that they'd seen him like they might with someone less recognizable, especially not since Noelle had apparently banned him from the spa.

"I better go before Noelle catches me out here. I'm supposed to be in the back getting ready for my first client." She flicked her hair back over her shoulder.

I could have tried to get her to stay and talk to me a little longer, but I didn't know what Noelle would think if she caught Amber hanging out in the hallway with me, so I just smiled and thanked her for talking to me.

She turned and looked me in the eye. It was the first time she had, since she was always playing with her hair. "Thanks for caring about Gina," she said then walked toward the spa entrance.

I turned to watch her go. Something about the way the door slammed behind her sounded ominous to me, but I shrugged it off.

I shoved it to the back of my mind and turned to Sandra. "So how are you doing?" I asked with a smile.

Her eyes flicked around, doing nothing to hide her anxiety. "I've been better." She smiled weakly.

I didn't know how much to play dumb and how much to let on that Mike had told me. I didn't want to say anything that could mess up his chances even more. I decided that the less I let on, the better. "Did you hear the spa reopened?"

She nodded slowly.

"Mike tells me you guys had a couples massage scheduled."

Another slow nod.

"So you still get to do it. That's great!" I hoped that if nothing else, my unabashed enthusiasm would sway her in favor of it.

It didn't work.

"I—I don't know if we're going to."

"Why not?" I asked, as if I didn't know.

She shrugged and looked around anywhere but at my face, far from the normal self-confident Sandra I'd known since we were kids. "I just don't feel comfortable, knowing that someone got killed down here yesterday and whoever did it is still on the loose."

"You know Mike would never let anyone hurt you."

She finally met my gaze with a look that said what she wouldn't—or couldn't.

"That's not it, is it?"

She looked away again as she shook her head.

Somehow I felt like it would have been easier to change her mind if she'd been afraid for her life instead of her heart.

"He loves you. You know that? He really wants this to work out," I said softly. I felt awkward and inappropriate, like I was simultaneously betraying a confidence and giving someone unwanted advice, which was probably actually a pretty good description of the situation. But I didn't know what else to do, with her standing there in front of me, looking nervous, like she was about to make the biggest decision of her life. And I'd never forgive myself if I didn't try.

"I know," she whispered. "The whole thing just seems like a bad sign. We come here to try again, and *this* happens? What if it's the universe telling me to move on? What if I ignore it and everything is worse than before? I just don't know what to do." She looked completely forlorn.

I didn't know what to say. On the one hand, I could just tell her to go for it—get back together with Mike. It would be great. They would live happily ever after. But what if I was wrong? Even though I wanted things to work out between them, I couldn't just blindly tell her that it was the right thing to do. After all, I didn't really know.

I reached out and rubbed her arm. "Follow your heart."

"But what if it's wrong?" She looked me in the eye, but I couldn't tell if she was afraid she was wrong for wanting to go back to him or leave for good.

I tried to look more confident than I felt. "It's never wrong to follow your heart."

For a second, I thought she thought it sounded as ridiculous as I was afraid it did. But after staring at me for what felt like a very long time but must have only been a few seconds, she reached out and pulled me into a big hug.

"Thank you, Fran," she said when she finally let me go. She actually looked happy.

"So you're going to get your massage?" If Sandra was going to go get the massage, I could stop worrying about solving Gina's murder. Not that I wanted her killer to go free, but it wouldn't be my problem anymore.

She hesitated, looking a little uneasy. "I don't know yet. I still need to think about it some more." She stopped and smiled. "But I feel better about it."

"Good," I said and smiled back at her.

"I better get back. Mike's going to be wondering where I disappeared to."

I considered it a good sign that she was concerned about Mike worrying about her. It was at least better than her avoiding him. She hadn't committed to the massage, but I felt like I'd at least put in a good effort that Mike would have to appreciate even if I hadn't figured out Gina's murder yet.

Chapter 20

AFTER SANDRA WENT BACK UP to her room, I stood in the hallway outside the spa for a few minutes, trying to decide my next move. I could try to talk to more of the girls who worked in the spa, but it didn't seem like most of the hotel guests had the same qualms about lounging at a murder scene that Sandra did. There was steady foot traffic into the spa as people came down to use their free spa day. Either that or they were just ghoulish sorts who wanted to check out the scene of the crime. Whatever their reasons for being down there, I didn't think I was going to have much opportunity to talk to any of the girls.

I sighed. Mike wouldn't be happy about it, but I was pretty sure there was nothing else I could do down there, not right now anyway. Maybe I could come back later, closer to closing time, and try my luck again. I decided to head back to the room and see what Matt was up to.

I walked slowly, letting my mind wander as I went. It was beyond frustrating that virtually no one had any information about what had happened to Gina, and on the rare occasion someone actually told me something useful—like that Garrett had it out for Gina—someone else contradicted it immediately, like how Carrick said that Garrett may have had a temper, but he wasn't a murderer. Sure, I knew a few more things about the soap opera–style drama of the Alford Inn, but I wasn't sure any of that shed light on Gina's murder. I was honestly at the point where I was beginning to think that either everyone knew who killed her and was keeping their mouths firmly closed or that her murderer was invisible.

I stopped dead in the middle of the hall and turned slowly back around to look at the housekeeping cart I'd just passed. It was the first one I'd seen since I'd been there. Or was it? Was the housekeeping staff extra covert here, or had I just not paid attention?

Who really noticed the housekeeping staff? Sure, I noticed their work—turning down our bed and making it back up again, cleaning the bathroom—but they'd seemed to operate invisibly, coming in and out of our room completely unobserved by us. And I suspected I wasn't the only one like that. House-keeping was practically meant to be invisible. And with the spa rooms having to be turned over between clients, surely there was housekeeping staff in there all the time. It was the perfect opportunity to commit murder—or the perfect cover.

"Excuse me." I poked my head into the utility room the housekeeping cart was standing outside of.

A middle-aged woman dressed in pale blue stepped around a corner, her arms laden with fluffy white robes. "Can I help you?"

"Um, yeah." I suddenly realized I would need to have some reason I had stopped to talk to her. I decided to go with my old reliable. "I was wondering if it would be possible to get some more towels?"

"Of course! What's your room number?"

I wanted to kick myself as I told her. If I kept this up, I'd have a room overflowing with towels.

"I'll get that taken care of for you." She picked up a tablet from the cart and started tapping on it. "I'm actually spa housekeeping, but I can get the request submitted to the guest room staff."

"Oh, I'm sorry. I didn't realize you were a separate department."

"Yup. Blue is spa. Light gray is guest rooms." She plucked at her scrubs-like uniform top, flashing me a wide toothy smile that was traced in a bright red a touch too orange for her pale skin. "Happens all the time."

At least now I knew she worked in the spa. "Can I ask you a question?"

I expected to see the curtain fall behind her eyes—the one that said she didn't want to talk about the murder. But instead, a little light went on. This was a woman who liked to gossip. But still, just in case I was reading her wrong, I wanted to ease into it.

"The treatment rooms in the spa—they get cleaned between each client, right?"

The disappointment on her face was obvious. She was apparently a woman who *really* liked to gossip. "Oh, of course. It wouldn't be sanitary otherwise. The health department would shut us right down."

I paused and leaned in, glancing up and down the hall for effect. "Were you working yesterday?"

The light came back on. She nodded rapidly. "Mm-hmm."

I took a conspiratorial step closer to her. "Did you see anything?"

"Ugh, no. I wish I had."

"Oh, that's too bad." I stepped back and sighed. "Do you think the police are going to catch whoever did it?"

She nodded confidently. "Definitely. I mean, they always do on the TV shows, don't they? And those are always in big cities like New York or LA. Or nationwide! This is just little podunk western Mass!"

I didn't have the heart to point out that those

shows were scripted. And that it wouldn't make very good TV if the good guys lost.

"Actually—" She leaned toward me. "There's a rumor that the hotel manager did it!"

Chalk up another point in the Garrett column. "Did anyone see him down there?"

She shook her head, looking disappointed. "And I've asked everybody! Well, almost everybody. There was a new girl working yesterday, and I haven't run into her again yet. Didn't catch her name either." She glanced down at her cart, looking glum before brightening up suddenly. "But you know what? If I don't, I'll just go ask Garrett who she was. I'll tell him that she misplaced something and I need to talk to her about it. Then he'll have to tell me who she is and where to find her. And he won't even know he's incriminating himself!" She put her hand on her hip and looked at me with a self-satisfied smile.

I wished she lived in Cape Bay. She had a shamelessness to her that would have come in handy in some of the murder cases I'd gotten involved in. Not that I was planning to ever do that again. But then again, I hadn't exactly planned on doing it in the past either.

"Are there any other rumors? Any good gossip?" I brushed my fingers against one of the robes she'd laid on top of the cart. It looked like normal terrycloth, but it was one of the softest things I'd ever touched. I wondered if I could get Matt down to the spa this afternoon. Assuming I didn't get a good lead from the housekeeper, of course.

She sighed. "Not really. Everyone was really surprised. Gina was a good kid. It's terrible what happened. Really terrible. With all the crazy folks who work in this hotel, I never would have guessed Gina would be the one to get knocked off."

I nodded sympathetically but thought it was a strange thing to say. "Are there some people you *would* have expected to be murdered?"

She hesitated, seeming to realize that she may have said something she shouldn't have. "Well," she said after a few seconds, "it's not that I thought anyone would kill them, but I know there wouldn't be too many sad faces if that nasty Sophie up in the bakery never came back. Have you met her? She's a real piece of work."

I couldn't say I was surprised. I didn't even work there, and I wouldn't be sorry if she just stopped showing up. As long as it wasn't because she was dead, of course.

"And, oh, have you met that boy who works the coffee bar? Carrot? Wouldn't be sad to see him go either."

I assumed she meant Carrick, although calling him Carrot amused me. I might have to start thinking of him that way whenever he annoyed me.

"Garrett—that's the hotel manager—if he took off, it wouldn't be a loss to anyone. But now, you know who I would miss? Tommy—the bartender. Mm-mm, he's a cutie, isn't he? And so nice and friendly! That Carrot could learn a thing or two from him."

I didn't disagree with her there. Tommy was definitely one of the more pleasant employees I'd met at the hotel.

"Well, I better get back to work." She pulled closed the door of the storage room. "The spa's packed today, between that free day they offered and all the looky-loos. If you ask me, they should have kept it closed. It doesn't seem right, being business as usual down there with Gina's killer on the loose."

I agreed and thanked her.

"They should have your extra towels up to your room later today. If you need them before that, just call down to the desk and let that Whitney girl know. She'll fix you up."

Oh right. The towels. I'd practically be able to start my own spa in the room with the number I'd have after I got even *more* delivered.

The spa housekeeper set off, trundling down the hall with her cart, and I turned to make my way back up to my room. Everything seemed to keep circling back to Garrett. I was starting to think that if it looked like a duck and it quacked like a duck, well, he must be a murderer. But I wasn't sure. And I knew Mike—and the local police—wouldn't go for "there's no evidence except some rumors pointing to him, but there's no evidence pointing to anyone else either!"

They wanted actual evidence, something they could take to a jury. Not wild guesses by the housekeeping staff. I was out of ideas, but maybe something would jump out at me on my way up.

Chapter 21

THE ELEVATOR DOORS opened on my floor, but I didn't get out. I was frozen in place. I had just had a stunning realization—the new spa housekeeper. It made so much sense.

There was a new housekeeper down in the spa yesterday. The maid I talked to saw her. And hadn't seen her since. It was possible that she'd decided not to come back after there was a murder her first day on the job, but it was also possible she wasn't employed there at all. I had to tell Mike. It wasn't much, but I had to tell him. I could have kicked myself for not getting a description though. He'd want that.

I thought for a second about going back down to the spa, but what would I say? "I need to talk to one of your housekeepers? Uh, middle-aged? Likes to gossip? Bright-red lipstick that's the wrong color for her skin tone?" It didn't seem promising, but maybe Mike could figure out how to talk to her again.

The elevator doors had closed, and I had to wait for the elevator to get up to the top floor, where someone had called it, before I could ride back down to my floor.

I actually got off when the elevator reached my floor this time and headed for my room. I wondered if it would be too much to stop off at Mike's room to tell him my housekeeper theory. He'd probably want to know, but I wasn't sure if he'd appreciate my stopping by unannounced. Still, he had a peephole—he didn't have to answer the door if he didn't want to.

As it turned out, when I turned the corner to the hallway where both our rooms were, someone else was already knocking on Mike's door. Unless I wanted to wait in line, it looked like talking to Mike was definitely out.

The person at the door was holding a tray—room service, I figured, although for some reason, I didn't feel confident about that.

I was close enough to hear when Sandra opened the door. She looked and sounded confused. "We didn't order anything."

"Oh, it's courtesy of the hotel. Because of everything that's happened."

The woman holding the tray sounded vaguely familiar, so I tried to get a look at her as I went by, but her long blond hair hung down on either side of her face, blocking my view. Still, something about her voice was so familiar and not in that vague "maybe she's someone I went to college with" kind of way— no, I felt like if I did know her, I'd heard her voice recently. But for the life of me, I couldn't figure out where.

"Um, okay. Thank you." Sandra took the tray from the girl and went back inside. I glanced over my shoulder to see if she was coming my way, but she was going straight down the hall, past the elevators. I figured the hotel must encourage employees to take the stairs when possible to leave the elevators for guests. Or maybe there was a service elevator down there.

I stopped outside my door and glanced back down the long hallway at the girl. She walked quickly, her loose blond curls bouncing on her back. I got a vague sense of déjà vu. But like all annoying cases of déjà vu, I couldn't place it.

I held my key to the magnetic lock and opened the door. "Matt. I'm back."

"Hey, Franny!"

I came around the corner and saw him still sprawled out on the couch, watching a couple of middle-aged men argue about who was the best—or maybe worst—at some position in some sport I didn't care enough to figure out.

"They delivered some coffee for you a little bit ago. It should still be warm."

I looked at the tray sitting on the table. It was identical to the one that had just been dropped off at Mike and Sandra's room. "Did you order that?"

Matt shook his head. "Nope. Girl just brought it by. Said it was from the hotel because of the murder."

I nodded slowly. Something about that felt wrong. Jacques had sent up that big box of macarons, and that hadn't felt strange to me. And they'd offered us a free day in the spa, so it wasn't the fact that they were trying to make up for our visit being marred by a murder. And the cost of a couple cups of coffee paled in comparison to either the macarons or the spa day, so it wasn't that either.

"You want me to warm up your coffee in the microwave?"

My nose wrinkled automatically. Microwaved coffee never tasted right to me.

Matt laughed. "Well, you were kind of just staring."

"I know," I said slowly, still looking at the tray. Something wasn't right, but what was it? "Did you drink any?"

"No, I wanted to let you pick first. She said one's a macchiato and one's a latte, and I know you like both, so I didn't want to pick the wrong one."

I nodded and turned to go to the bathroom.

"Are you going to drink this? Which one do you want?"

"Just pick whichever." I was too distracted to pick which drink I wanted, especially without looking at them and smelling them.

It did seem strange that they were bringing up the trays individually instead of using a cart. But maybe they were afraid that the last ones to be delivered would be cold before they ever got to their destinations. I stepped into the bathroom and saw that a fresh stack of towels had joined the others.

My heart stopped.

The girl at Mike and Sandra's door had been wearing head-to-toe light blue—a spa maid's uniform. And spa maids weren't room service.

"Don't drink that!" I screamed, running back over to Matt.

He'd just opened one of the cups and was holding it to his mouth.

"Don't drink that!" I repeated.

"Okay?" He put it down slowly. "Can I have the other one?"

"No!" I knocked them both over, just to make sure he didn't have a choice but to listen to me, then spun on my heel and ran out of the room and down the hall. I stopped at Mike's door and pounded on it. "Mike! Open the door! Sandra! Mike! Open the door!"

"What's going on?" Matt had stuck his head out

of our door and was looking at me like I'd lost my mind, but I didn't care. I kept banging on the door and yelling for Mike and Sandra.

What was taking them so long to open it? I began to wonder if I could convince Whitney to let me in and if it would be too late by then. "Mike!"

The door jerked open. "Fran! What the hell?" He somehow managed to look even more annoyed than I'd ever seen him—and he had been pretty annoyed with me a time or two. He was also missing his shirt, but I didn't have time to wonder right then if his irritation was due to me interrupting a romantic reunion.

"Don't drink the coffee. Whatever you do, don't drink it!" I ran down the hall before he had a chance to do anything but look at me like he was worried about my sanity.

"What the hell?" I heard him say again behind me.

"I don't know, man." Matt must have wandered down to see why I was freaking out. "At least she didn't slap it out of your hand."

The girl I'd seen at Mike and Sandra's door was gone now, but I hoped I could catch her in the stairs. I had to catch her. But, if I didn't, at least I might be able to describe her to someone and figure out who she was—and if she was really supposed to be delivering coffee to guests. Those long, shiny blond curls she had would be enough to identify her. People notice gorgeous hair like that.

It was a very long hallway, but I got to the end and jerked open the heavy fire door. And stopped and stared.

There, on the landing just inside the door, was a pale-blue spa maid uniform. And next to it, a long, wavy blond wig.

Chapter 22

I WRUNG MY HANDS TOGETHER. I couldn't help it. I couldn't stop myself, even when Matt grabbed one of my hands and tried to hold it still. I just rubbed his hand with the one he'd grabbed and grated my fingernails up and down my leg with the other. I'd be lucky if I didn't have bruises in the morning.

Sandra, sitting on the couch across from me, looked like a statue. The polar opposite of my anxious fidgeting, she sat perfectly still, but every muscle in her body held a tension that looked like she might jump up and fly screaming out of the hotel at any moment.

"There's Mike."

I looked up and followed Matt's eyes across the lounge to Mike walking in from the lobby. He was, fortunately, wearing a shirt now. Two, actually. A white T-shirt with a blue flannel over it. His hands were shoved in his pockets in a way that I was sure was meant to convey an attitude of casual relaxation, but as he walked toward us, his unbuttoned flannel shirt shifted slightly, and I caught sight of the butt of a gun on his hip.

He sat down next to Sandra and took her hand. She didn't move, not even her eyes, which were trained on a spot on the floor somewhere between us.

Mike looked from Matt to me to Sandra, his eyes lingering on his wife a little longer than on me or Matt. Then he took a deep, controlled breath and, in a voice so low I had to strain to hear it, filled us in on what the local police had just told him.

"They confirmed the presence of large doses of opioids in all four cups."

If Sandra had looked before like she wanted to run screaming, I was pretty sure that now Mike's hand holding hers was the only thing keeping her from doing it.

"The ones in your room were a little harder to test, of course, since they were splattered all over the floor, but they managed to get enough from what hadn't spilled out to test them individually." He gave me a look that seemed to be part admiration and part amusement at my near-hysterical reaction.

Matt squeezed my hand tighter.

"They need to run some more tests, but they're pretty sure it was fentanyl."

I searched his eyes, trying to figure out if he could really be saying what I thought he was saying.

"With the amount that was in them, one sip would have been enough to kill any of us."

Sandra's body jerked, and Matt leaned his head into his free hand and muttered an obscenity under his breath.

"Fran saved all of our lives."

It was the kind of thing he normally would have looked pained to say. He never liked to admit that I'd helped him out with a case or been right about anything, especially when he felt like I was acting more on gut instinct than on logic and evidence, which to be fair, I usually was. But at this moment, there was none of that. He met my eyes with unabashed gratitude for acting on my instincts—even if they made me look crazy—and saving his life. And his wife's.

Matt rubbed his forehead. "Why would anyone try to kill Fran? And you?"

"Well, the obvious answer is that I'm a police officer, and Fran has been openly asking a lot of questions about the case. Whoever it was must have thought we were getting too close for comfort and decided to do something about it." Mike stopped and took a deep breath. There was something else, but he seemed hesitant to say it. "But we don't think I was the second target."

I stared at Mike, confused. Yes, Matt had talked to

Tommy and Carrick about the murder earlier that day, but was that really enough for someone to think he needed to die? Surely it was a prime topic of conversation among all of the guests. And something else—"Then why deliver poisoned coffee to your room?"

Mike looked at me with something I'd never seen behind his eyes. His jaw clenched. "To kill Sandra."

For the first time since we'd sat down, Sandra moved. She looked up at Mike with wide eyes. "Me?"

His jaw tensed again, and his head bobbed in the slightest nod.

"But why kill Sandra?" I asked too loudly for the room and the conversation.

The few other people in the room looked up as Mike glared at me. I realized what that look in his eye was—it was fury. Fury that someone had tried to kill him, kill his friends. Kill his wife. And at the moment, it was fury at me for practically yelling something that I should have whispered. But as soon as it flared, he got it under control. I might have been stupid, but I wasn't the enemy, and he knew that.

"You and Sandra were talking this afternoon? In the hallway outside the spa?"

I nodded.

"About the murder?"

This time, I shook my head. "No."

Mike's eyebrows rose. He didn't believe me. He

thought I was lying, blatantly, to his face, in front of someone who could easily contradict me and tell the truth.

But she didn't. Because it was the truth.

"No," I said again. "Maybe just for a second in passing, but only because we were talking about the spa opening back up and the massage you were scheduled for. And about y—" I stopped as Sandra suddenly looked over at me. She didn't want me to say. Didn't want me to tell Mike that she and I had been discussing their marriage. Fair enough. "We were talking about the massage."

Mike's face went from two eyebrows raised to just one, but he still didn't believe me. Maybe a little more than before, but he knew I was still hiding something.

I kept my mouth shut, my chin raised in defiance. If Sandra didn't want me to tell, I wouldn't tell.

"You were overheard talking about it."

I wanted to protest that whoever was claiming that was the real liar, but then realization dawned. "No, I was talking to Amber. Who works down in the spa. She was the one who found the body."

Mike's brows knit together, and I knew why. Sandra and Amber looked nothing alike. Sandra was a natural blonde, while Amber had dark hair. Sandra wore street clothes while I'd never seen Amber in anything but spa white. Sandra probably wasn't quite old enough to be Amber's mother, but if she wasn't, she would have had to be a much older sister. They couldn't be mistaken for each other.

"I was talking to Amber about it when Sandra came by. I stopped her so I could talk to her for a minute. Whoever thought we were talking about the murder must have seen the three of us together and heard something about the murder and thought Sandra was involved in the conversation too."

Mike looked at Sandra, who nodded. "She's telling the truth," she said softly.

Mike gave a curt nod. The muscles in his jaw flexed as he clenched his teeth. I knew what he must have been thinking. Here he was, trying to rekindle things with his wife and get a murder investigation wrapped up before it was too late for them, and he practically got his wife killed in the process. Or at least that was what I assumed he was thinking. He may have just been trying not to be mad that he was wrong about what happened.

"So you said it was Amber you talked to?"

"Yes."

"I'll let the local guys know. They may need to pull her aside for her own safety. Or for questioning."

A chill went down my spine at the thought of Amber possibly being a suspect. She'd seemed genuinely devastated by her friend's death and genuinely interested in finding out who killed her—unless that was all an act. That possibility terrified me.

We sat in silence as Mike got up and went to talk

to the police in the lobby. When he got back, he sat down and rubbed his hand across the back of his neck. "They don't think she's involved but said they'll pull her in just in case."

Just in case she was a murderer or a potential victim, he didn't say.

We sat for another minute before Matt spoke up. "So, what do we do now?"

Mike inhaled slowly. "The local guys say we're free to leave, especially since there was an attempt on all of our lives. It would probably be a good idea."

I had to admit it was tempting to flee the hotel and forget all about this nightmare of a vacation. But if someone was trying to kill me, it had to be because I was onto something. And I wasn't going to back down. My wits had saved us all. Maybe they could lead me to whoever did it too. "I'm not leaving."

All three of their heads swiveled toward me.

"I'm sorry?" Mike asked.

"Are you joking, Franny?" Matt looked incredulous.

I shook my head. "I'm not leaving. I'm seeing this through."

Mike shook his head, but he knew better than to argue. Once I'd made up my mind, I wasn't changing it.

Matt knew that too. "Well, then, I guess I'm staying too."

Mike's jaw clenched again. "I can't leave the two

of you alone here." He looked at Sandra, who looked like she thought we'd all lost our minds. "You can go. No one will blame you," he said softly.

She hesitated before shaking her head. "No, I'll stay."

"Baby, I——" He put his hand on her cheek and ducked his head down. Whatever he said to her was too quiet for me to hear.

She looked unsure, but I thought she was about to agree when the lights flickered, followed almost immediately by a crash of thunder that shook the whole hotel.

The sky had gotten cloudy earlier, but I hadn't expected rain until sheets of it suddenly started pouring down, accompanied by a massive gust of wind.

Tommy and Carrick, who had been behind their respective bars, both rushed out and over to the wall of windows, closing them as fast as they could but still getting drenched in the process.

Sandra shook her head. "No. I'm not driving in that. Not in the dark and not somewhere I'm not familiar with."

Mike nodded. I could tell he didn't want her driving in a storm like that either. It might have been risky staying in the hotel when a murderer had his sights set on us, but driving down twisting mountain roads while being buffeted by gale-force winds and torrential rain had the potential to be even more dangerous.

For a moment, we sat there, letting it sink in that we were staying—because we wanted to or because four strong walls seemed safer than a metal box on wet, curvy roads—in a place where someone had tried to kill us—all four of us—just hours before. And we were clearly targets, but we didn't know whose target we were. It wasn't exactly how I expected the weekend to go.

"Is anybody else hungry? You guys want to get something to eat? We could go by one of the restaurants—" Matt, perpetually thinking of his stomach, started to ask before Mike cut him off.

"We're not eating or drinking anything prepared inside this hotel."

I almost asked why, but then I realized—we had successfully evaded one attempt to kill us by poisoning our food, but we might not be so lucky a second time. I hadn't been the slightest bit hungry before, more concerned about who had tried to murder us, but at the prospect of not eating until at least the next day, my stomach suddenly started to rumble.

"We could go out," Matt suggested.

Sandra glanced over her shoulder at the storm and shuddered.

I didn't want to go out in it either. "We have some macarons in our room," I offered. The sugary treats weren't particularly substantial nutrition, but it might subdue the hunger pangs until we could make it out.

"From the bakery?" Mike asked.

I nodded.

"Were you there when they were packed?"

I thought about it. I was pretty sure we'd gone through the small box that I'd picked, but we still had the other—that had been sent up to our room. "No, but we've already had some and—"

"No. We can't risk it. The suspect could have poisoned just one. It's actually the smarter way to do it."

"They were from Jacques." Mike's tone had left no room for objection, but I held onto some fragile hope that he would change his mind if I just explained the circumstances.

He did not appreciate my comment. "How do you know that?"

"The card—"

"Could have been written and signed by anyone. He could have written it and had someone else pack them. He could have packed them and passed them off to someone else to deliver. If anyone had even a moment where they were alone with them—or not even alone, just where they could tamper with them without being noticed—they could have added the drugs. We're not eating them."

This time, I didn't argue.

I was beginning to resign myself to the possibility

of going hungry for the night when Matt's stomach decided to intervene again.

"What if just one of us went out? We could pick something up from a place in town and bring it back to eat here."

To my surprise, Mike didn't immediately shoot him down. Instead he looked thoughtful for a moment before slowly nodding. "That could work. But no one goes out alone. It's too risky. We have to stay in pairs."

"I'll go with him." It only made sense. Matt was my boyfriend, and Mike clearly didn't want to leave Sandra.

Mike looked like he was about to agree but then stood up and shook his head. "No. You stay. I'll go."

Sandra looked up at him in alarm.

"I'm a better driver."

"I'm a good driver!" Matt protested.

Mike rolled his eyes and, for a second, dropped his in-charge police persona and was just like any other of Matt's friends. "Come on. I'm a cop, man."

Matt grudgingly conceded.

"Do you want to come with me or stay here?" Mike asked, looking down at Sandra.

She looked at him with anguish in her eyes. I could see her waver back and forth before setting her jaw in resolve. "I'll stay. Just in case—" Her shoulder twitched, and her lip quivered. "The kids."

Mike's face fell, and I thought he was going to change his mind. Sandra wanted to make sure that the kids had one parent left if the car went skidding off the road, but it looked like, to Mike's mind, two parents were better than one. Which wasn't wrong, although given what I knew about my father, I had probably been better off with just my mother. Mike, on the other hand, was devoted to his kids.

"I can go," I offered again. I even stood up to show that I wasn't just saying it to be nice. Matt and I had less to lose. It hurt me to think of how sad Latte would be if we never came home, but I had no doubt that Sammy would take excellent care of him. I loved him like my child, but I'd never be able to look at Mike and Sandra's kids if I knew I could have taken their dad's place.

Mike appeared to consider it and spent a long few seconds looking into Sandra's eyes. It was the kind of silent conversation I'd seen between only a few of my married friends, and I hoped they knew how special it was that they understood each other that way.

My resolve strengthened. I patted Matt on the shoulder. "Let's go."

Matt had just stood up and turned toward the door when Mike put out his arm to stop me from following.

"No." He looked at Matt. "You might be a good driver, but we stand the best chance of making it back alive if I go."

Matt shrugged, and I could tell his mind was more

on his stomach than who was going with him to get the food to fill it.

"Take care of Sandra," Mike whispered as he walked past me, and I wasn't sure if he meant for the hour or so they might be gone or if he didn't make it back.

Chapter 23

SANDRA and I made a few weak efforts at conversation but kept falling back into silence. We were both too far into our own minds, thinking about what had almost happened to us and what could happen to the men in our lives, to actually keep it up.

I tried to project confidence for her sake, but I wasn't sure if I was successful. Definitely not if I had to genuinely feel it. I was beyond worried. What if, despite Mike's driving abilities, he ran off the road and killed them both? What if whoever had tried to kill us that afternoon tried again during the night, when we were asleep?

Maybe I needed to suggest all of us crashing in one room and taking turns on watch. Knowing Mike and Matt, they wouldn't stand for that and would work out a scheme where they never woke me or Sandra for our turn. Of course, knowing Mike, he probably wouldn't wake Matt either and would just sit up the entire night, watching to make sure all of us were safe.

But first they had to get back.

"Are you as nervous as I am?" Sandra asked after a while.

I straightened my shoulders and tried to look relaxed. But as soon as I met her eyes, I crumbled. "I don't think I've ever been this worried in my life."

She chuckled softly. "You know, he goes out there every day and risks his life. They tell you that all the time—that when your husband is a cop, you never know if he won't make it home one night. But it's Cape Bay. I always worry, but I can ignore it. I can usually block it out. Focus on the kids, focus on work, paint my nails or something."

Her voice dropped a little more. "That was part of it, you know. I mean, it wasn't that. It was part of it, though. Just the stress of whether he was coming home every day. It wears on you." She made a noise that sounded like a hiccup but I suspected, by the sudden wateriness of her eyes, was more her choking back a sob. "It didn't help. I worry about him just as much. Maybe more since we don't talk during his shift and he doesn't call when he gets home unless he wants to talk to the kids, so I don't really know that he's okay. I just have to tell myself that no news is good news and keep on going for the sake of the kids. Sometimes I think it's going to break me."

She looked at me, and the tears in her eyes were unmistakable now. "I still love him, Fran. I do. I'm just so afraid all the time, and sometimes I think I'd be better off finding someone else with a nice stable office job—someone like Matt—and settling down with him so I at least know that the kids will have someone if they lose their father."

I couldn't help but notice that she was worried about the kids having someone and not her.

"I'm just so scared, Fran." She covered her face with her hands and started to cry.

I moved over to the sofa next to her and put my arm around her shoulder.

She calmed down after a few minutes and wiped her eyes. "I'm sorry. I don't know what came over me. I'm sorry."

I patted her arm. "Don't feel bad. It's fine. It's totally fine."

She took a deep, shaky breath and nodded. "I'm going to go to the restroom to splash some cold water on my face." She only took two steps before stopping and looking back at me. "Do you think that's safe? For me to go alone?"

I thought about it for a second and nodded. So far, the only attacks had been in private places—a treatment room at the spa and our rooms. No one had been assaulted in a public place. The bathroom wasn't exactly public, but it wasn't secluded either. Even so, I understood if she was uneasy. "I can go with you if you want."

She stood up a little straighter, and I could tell she was trying to be brave. "No, I'll be fine."

"I'll watch the door for you." I actually felt like that was safer than me following her. There weren't a ton of people in the lobby, but Tommy and Carrick were both back behind their bars, and this way I felt like I could make sure no one else went into the restroom after her.

The bathrooms were down a short hallway, but I could see both doors from where I sat. I watched and waited until she came back a couple of minutes later, looking somewhat refreshed if not totally back to normal.

"Mind watching while I go in there real quick?" I asked.

"Go right ahead."

I could tell she was still on edge. I hesitated to leave her, but I really had to go, so I scurried over to the restroom and ducked in. It was the swanky kind of bathroom where the stall doors fitted snugly into real doorframes and went almost to the floor, offering the occupants some measure of privacy. I walked down past all of the stalls, making sure I was alone. Satisfied that I was, I ducked into one, did what I needed to do, and came back out to wash my hands.

I was just about to leave when a white-hot pain

slammed into the back of my head, sending me stumbling toward the door with stars in my eyes.

Before I could even figure out what had happened, someone grabbed a handful of hair at the back of my head, jerked me backward, then drove me headfirst into the wall. My forehead crashed into the drywall just above the tile.

There was a noise like screaming, but I wasn't sure if it was me or the ringing in my ears.

I felt myself being dragged backward and fought to get away. I could barely stay on my feet, but I tried to sling an elbow at whoever it was. I barely made contact and tried again. This time, I missed completely.

My assailant slung me around and slammed me into the wall between two of the stalls. Somehow, I didn't appreciate the bathroom's solid construction as much as I had earlier.

I reached behind my head and dug my fingernails into the hand grasping my hair.

A feminine voice screamed. This time, it definitely wasn't me. "I'm going to kill you!"

For the moment, I was free. I ran for the door, but she grabbed me again, this time by my shirt.

I spun around as best I could, throwing my elbow. I connected with her cheekbone, and she screamed. As her face swung away from me, her short black hair swung around her face. Sophie!

But something didn't make sense—when she said

it, she didn't have a trace of a French accent. Then it hit me—the blonde who had delivered the poisoned coffee was the same as the blonde I'd seen upstairs, who I'd thought was sneaking into the rooms with her boyfriend. And the reason I'd thought they both sounded familiar was because it was Sophie, just without her accent.

"It was you!" I screamed.

"You're just now figuring that out? I thought you were onto me a long time ago. Why else would you keep hanging around me all the time?" She spat the words out at me, sounding more Southern than French now.

"Because I like macarons!" And now they'd probably be ruined for me. For some reason, knowing she was responsible for all this made me even angrier. And now that I was finally facing her, I could use some of what I'd learned in the kickboxing classes I'd been taking instead of just twisting and flailing.

Hoping to catch her off guard, I kicked and caught her in the midsection. She lunged at me. I dodged away, but she caught my shoulder, knocking me into the sharp edge of the sink. She ran toward me again, and this time I managed to hit her with both my foot and my fist. She stumbled backward, clutching her hands against her nose. I could see blood beginning to leak down past her palms.

If she hadn't been between me and the door, I would have run. But there was no exit without going past Sophie. She looked like she was in a lot of pain from where I'd presumably broken her nose, but I didn't trust her for a second.

I ran the few steps toward her, grabbed her by the wrists, and spun her around so that I was between her and the door. Then I shoved her as hard as I could. She stumbled backward, hit the far wall, and sank to the floor.

She wasn't unconscious—or at least I didn't think she was—so as much as I wanted to run for my life, I was afraid she'd grab me before I made it two steps out the door. Instead, I watched her and inched toward the door while trying to catch my breath.

I was about to reach for the door when I noticed that she wasn't quite as slumped as she had been. I glanced over to grab the handle, and by the time I looked back, she was on her feet.

I needed to get out. Now.

I turned to go for the door just as she ran at me again, screeching like a madwoman.

The door burst open before I could get to it, and Mike came barreling through with Matt on his heels.

Mike stuck his arm out and had Sophie facedown on the floor with her hands behind her back before I even knew he had caught her.

"Franny! Are you okay?" Matt pulled me into his arms and held me tight. He glanced over at Mike as he ratcheted handcuffs around Sophie's wrists. "Come on, let's go."

He opened the door and let me lead the way out into the lobby.

"Where's Sandra?" I asked, glancing around. She wasn't on the couch where I'd left her, and I didn't see her anywhere else in the lounge either. "Did she go up to the room?"

"What do you mean? She was right——" Matt stopped and looked around the lounge, appearing as confused as I felt.

A knife of fear stabbed my chest. "Sandra!" I ran out to the lobby, hoping she'd just wandered out there to look for the police or something. There was no one there except Whitney at the desk. I spun around in a circle, trying to figure out where she could have gone. Then a noise like a muffled scream made me look down the hall.

There, at the end, I caught sight of Sandra just as she was dragged around the corner.

"Get Mike!" I took off at a full sprint down the hall after Sandra and whoever had her.

"Where are you going?" Matt yelled after me. He hadn't caught sight of Sandra being dragged away.

"To get Sandra! Call 911!"

They had a good head start on me, but I didn't have a kicking and screaming woman holding back. I did have pure terror pushing me forward. I didn't know who had grabbed Sandra or what they planned to do with her, but after the way Sophie had attacked me, I didn't think they wanted to take her for a casual stroll in the gardens. I had no doubt that Sophie would have killed me in that bathroom if she could have, and I was afraid that was what was in store for Sandra, too, if I didn't get to her in time.

I reached the point where the hallway turned and led toward the back doors of the hotel. Almost to the glass doors at the end, a man had ahold of Sandra.

My first instinct was to yell, but I was afraid the man would move faster if he knew someone was on his tail. On the other hand, I didn't want Sandra to think no one knew she was gone. The contrasting thoughts flew through my head at lightning speed, and without consciously deciding, I yelled out, "Stop!"

The man glanced over his shoulder and lurched toward the door.

Sandra's eyes were wild as she saw me. She twisted in his grasp, and the man's grip loosened on her as he tried to get the door open. She managed to get her mouth free. "Fran!"

I ran as fast as I could toward her, my only thought being that I had to save her. I couldn't let Mike down.

Sandra and the man were outside and halfway down the wide stone stairs to the courtyard before I made it to the doors. He'd managed to grab a lounge chair and throw it in my way, but I jumped on top of it and used it to launch myself to the top of the stairs.

My momentum made me stumble as I started down them, but I fought to stay on my feet. I was getting closer. I had to get to her. I wasn't sure what I would do when I did, but I couldn't let him take her away from the hotel or to a more secluded area to kill her.

"Stop!" I screamed again.

We were in the courtyard near the big stone balcony off the lounge. I had to get to them before we got away from the hotel's lights. "Stop!"

I saw movement up on the balcony and prayed that someone had called for help and they weren't just watching a woman being kidnapped.

"Stop!" This time, someone else yelled it.

The new voice startled the man so much that he paused to look where it was coming from. But he didn't look up. And so he didn't see the body dropping off the balcony and landing on top of him.

I screamed. Sandra screamed.

The person who had come from the sky punched Sandra's kidnapper with a hit that knocked him out.

The man from the sky jumped up and grabbed Sandra around the waist, pulling her against him.

For a second, I thought it was yet another attacker, but then the light fell on his face, and I realized that the man who could have killed himself by diving off a balcony onto a stone patio was Mike.

Sandra must have realized it, too, because she flung her arms around his neck and kissed him.

Chapter 24

"SO LET ME GET THIS STRAIGHT." Matt leaned back on the couch and tented his fingers. "Tommy was in on it all along. Sophie's not French. They were selling drugs in the hotel, and they killed Gina because she found out and was going to turn them in to the police. Does that about cover it?"

I nodded and tried to relax my aching body into the comfortable-looking, plush armchair I'd claimed in the lobby lounge. It was the morning after Sophie and Tommy had tried to kill me and Sandra, and every bone and muscle in my body hurt.

After the first hit Sophie had landed in the bathroom the night before, I hadn't felt a thing, but when I woke up again, after finally falling into bed sometime after the sun came up, I could barely move. Matt had pried me from the bed only after dosing me with a large macchiato and a handful of painkillers—

legal, legitimate, over-the-counter painkillers, although if I'd gone to the hospital like the EMTs suggested when they checked me over after every-thing had settled down the night before, I might have had something stronger. As it was, I could barely move and had only managed to drag myself out of bed and down the stairs when Matt promised me as much coffee as I could handle and whatever food I felt like eating.

I could still hardly believe what had happened the night before. If not for the pain that wracked my body from head to toe, I would have found it easier to believe that I'd imagined it. How crazy was it that someone had tried to poison me, murder me in a bathroom, and kidnap Sandra—and that Mike had saved her by jumping off a balcony. It was the kind of thing that would happen in an action movie, not in my life. And speaking of action movies, why didn't they ever show how sore the hero was the next day? I dreaded the thought of getting in the car and driving the three plus hours back home.

"Did you ever have a clue Tommy was involved?" Matt asked.

"I never had a clue that *Sophie* was involved."

And I hadn't. If Tommy and Sophie hadn't panicked and tried to kill us, they probably would have been able to go on their merry way, selling their opioids with no one the wiser that they'd killed Gina. But they'd lost their cool and would now more than likely spend the rest of their lives in prison. And I was glad. They deserved it.

It had all come out the night before, after the police arrived, after Mike flew off the balcony in an effort to save his wife. I still didn't understand how it had been successful.

The Alford Inn wasn't the first upscale hotel where Tommy and Sophie had set up shop, but it was the place where they'd stayed the longest and been the most successful. For years now, they'd gone from resort to resort, getting jobs where they dealt with—and to—a lot of people.

Tommy had always worked in the restaurants and bars because he really was naturally friendly and an excellent bartender, while Sophie had started out as a waitress, moved into spas, and finally landed in bakeries when she figured out that a little extra white powder blended in quite nicely with all the sugar and flour. Her line about staying out of the patisserie kitchen had just been a lie to give her plausible deniability if anyone found her stash.

It had all gone well for them—they were moving loads of drugs and making money hand over fist—until Gina caught them sneaking out of a spa treatment room one day the week before we arrived. They probably could have played it off except for Sophie's wig and spa uniform—and the fact that she'd dropped her French accent and Gina had heard her using her real Texan one.

Oh, and Tommy and Sophie weren't Tommy and Sophie at all. Tommy was really named Adam and Sophie was really Sophia, which was at least closer. She'd changed it when she adopted the French accent, thinking it made her cover story more realistic. And they both had rap sheets as long as an arm, back in Texas.

When the local detective got ahold of those and showed them to us, Sandra and I realized just how lucky we'd been. Gina hadn't been the first person Tommy/Adam and Sophie/Sophia had killed, and the two of us wouldn't have been the last. I wasn't sure whether I felt comforted that we'd gotten away or terrified by how close we'd come to dying.

"Can I get either of you another drink?" Carrick asked, appearing beside us. He'd been exceptionally nice to both of us since we'd set foot in the lounge. It was like he was another person.

Matt looked at me, and I tried to shake my head but stopped because it hurt. "No."

"Are you sure? I can make you an espresso macchiato or a cappuccino or just a straight espresso shot?"

I flicked my eyes toward Carrick, momentarily wondering if he was a part of the drug operation, too, and was making a last-ditch effort to kill me, but I knew the police had interviewed him the night before and searched both bars thoroughly and found nothing to implicate anyone else.

"Okay, that's fine." He turned to go then stopped and came back. "Um, I wanted to say I'm sorry for being a jerk before. Tommy—Adam, whoever—made me nervous. He was charming to customers, but whenever we were alone, he acted like a bully. I started acting aggressive to protect myself. I probably should have cooled it around customers, but I was afraid he'd see through me if I did. You, uh, you really know your coffee." He bounced his head a little and started back toward the coffee bar. He was halfway there before I managed to make my mouth work.

"Hey, Carrick?"

He turned around.

"Actually, I would like something."

His face lit up. "Sure! Of course. What can I get you? I'll make you anything—whatever you want. On the house too. Since I was such a jerk before."

"Make me your favorite thing." It wasn't something I would normally say, not unless I knew the barista well and trusted their judgement. It was a compliment of the highest order—letting the person know you understood and respected their talent. Oddly, it wasn't something I actually liked customers to say since tastes varied so widely, but when a real coffee connoisseur came through, someone who I knew knew their coffee, it was an honor.

Carrick understood the code and stood up a little straighter. "Sure thing. I'll be right back."

Matt raised an eyebrow at me. I never let people pick my drink for me.

I shrugged before I remembered how much my shoulders hurt. "Deep down, I think he's a good kid."

He looked skeptical.

Under other circumstances, I might have tried to turn it into an engineering analogy that might make more sense to him—like letting someone else draft the first plans for a new project—but I ached and didn't feel much like talking any more than I had to.

I closed my eyes and tried to relax my sore muscles while I waited for my coffee. If nothing else, I could use the cup as a warm compress.

"Excuse me, Mr. Cardosi, Ms. Amaro."

I opened my eyes to see who was disturbing me. Garrett. He may not have been a murderer after all, but I still wasn't thrilled to see him.

He gave a wan smile. "I wanted to let you know that I've spoken with the owner of the hotel, and he is horrified about the experience you and your friends have had during your visit."

I supposed I should have thought that was nice, but if he'd felt anything other than horrified about how our visit had gone, I wouldn't think he should own a hotel.

"In an effort to make it up to you, he's offering both you and the Stantons the opportunity to extend your stay by another four days—fully comped, of course, including all meals, spa services, and your original stay."

Matt and I exchanged a glance.

"Furthermore, he'd like to invite you to return anytime, at your convenience, for a full week, with the same conditions. It will be entirely covered by the owner himself, including an upgraded room."

Surely he was joking. Of course, I had been almost killed…

"And he asked me to give you this. Everything I just described will be noted in the computer, but it's also documented here, along with a personal note from the owner." He handed the envelope to Matt, who looked inside and gave a low whistle. "Unfortunately," Garrett continued, "I won't be here after today. I'm moving on to another property, and someone else will be taking my place. However, please accept my sincere apologies for your troubles and my best wishes for the future." He gave a small bow and whisked himself away.

I glanced at Matt.

He shrugged. "Seems like a win to me."

Normally, I would have laughed, but laughing hurt.

"You want to stay an extra few days?"

I knew I needed to get back to the café. I had a million things to do back there, and despite Sammy's reassurances that everything was going well, I knew she was probably ready for a break from being in charge. But Matt had brought me out here so we could have some couple time without work and our usual home stresses getting in the way, and with Gina's murder and everything that had happened, we really hadn't had that yet. So I nodded. "Yeah, let's stay a couple more days."

I knew I'd made the right choice when he hopped up with a big grin on his face. "Great! I'll go let the front desk know."

Carrick returned with my coffee a moment after Matt walked away and handed it to me. I hesitated for a second, afraid it would be terrible and my face would show it. But then I took a deep breath and a big sip. It was delicious.

My face must have shown that because Carrick grinned. "It's a macchiato latte—I know you said you like the regular macchiatos, but I thought you might want something a little less intense this morning. I used my favorite beans from Panama and used a little less milk than usual and added my secret ingredient—cinnamon. And a little bit of Irish cream. I figured you could use it."

"It's really good. Thank you."

He grinned and headed back to the coffee bar.

"You want to head back upstairs so you can lie down?" Matt asked when he came back.

I didn't want to get up, but stretching out in that comfortable bed did sound appealing. Slowly, I nodded.

He took the coffee from me and helped me up, then let me lean on him as I shuffled down the hall.

I glanced inside the patisserie as we passed. It looked sad and empty. When Jacques had arrived around four to begin baking for the day and found out what Sophie had done, he threw everything in the bakery in the trash, from the delicious-looking tartes in the front windows to all his ingredients in the back. He said he didn't trust a thing she had touched. As soon as that was done, shortly before I got to bed, he had gone out to restock as best he could from the local grocery store.

"Mademoiselle! Mademoiselle Francesca!" Jacques called, popping out of the door to the kitchen as we passed. He held a small box in his hand. "I make these macarons fresh this morning. They are not as good as if they were aged a day or two, but I want you to have them. You are staying a few days, *non*? I will bring you more when I have them." He held the box out to me.

I took it and opened it. "Raspberry?"

"*Oui*. Raspberry *et chocolat*."

I took one out and bit into it. Aged or not, it was heaven. Even Sophie couldn't ruin macarons for me. "Thank you. It's delicious."

Matt reached over and grabbed one, stuffing the whole thing in his mouth. He grunted and nodded.

I laughed but only for a second. The spot where

Sophie had slammed my ribs into the edge of the sink objected.

I thanked Jacques again, and Matt and I resumed our slow trek upstairs. At least I could lean against the wall and rest for a minute in the elevator.

We reached our floor and started the walk down the long hall to our hotel room.

Halfway there, the door to Mike's room opened, and he came out, holding an ice bucket. "How you holding up there, Franny?"

I grimaced. "Been better. How's Sandra?"

"She's okay."

I wondered what "okay" meant. I wondered if they'd talked about their relationship and where it was going. I wondered if Mike's flying leap had helped her make up her mind.

"Garrett tell you guys about our visits getting comped and the extra days?" Matt asked.

Mike nodded but didn't say anything else. I would have walked away and let it be, but Matt didn't.

"So are you guys going to stay? Have you talked to Sandra?"

Mike's jaw tightened, and my stomach clenched. I was afraid it was bad news.

But then he looked at me, and one corner of his mouth turned up. I knew what he really meant when he finally answered.

"Sandra said she'll stay."

Recipe 1: Espresso Macchiato

Ingredients:
- Coffee beans/grounds for espresso
- Milk

You do need an espresso maker for this. Make a shot of espresso and pour it into your cup. Steam milk. The ideal temperature is 140° F (60° C). Pour steamed milk over the espresso and add dollop of foam on top.

Remember the espresso goes in first, followed by the milk.

Option to top the drink with whipped cream, grated chocolate, and/or cinnamon.

Recipe 2: Latte Macchiato

This is similar to the espresso macchiato but with more steamed milk, so use a tall glass. Another difference is the milk goes in the cup first, followed by the espresso.

Fill most of glass with steamed milk. Pour a shot of espresso over it. That's it!

The espresso settles between the layer of milk and the foam, resulting in three distinct layers.

Makes about 15 macarons

Macaron Shells:

- 1 cup ground almonds, sifted (or almond meal/almond flour)
- 1/2 cup powdered sugar, heaped and sifted
- 2 egg whites
- 5 tbsp granulated sugar
- 1 teaspoon lemon zest
- ½ teaspoon lemon juice
- Yellow gel food coloring

Lemon Buttercream:

- 3 tbsp unsalted butter, softened
- 1 cup powdered sugar
- 2 teaspoons heavy cream
- 1 tablespoon lemon juice

- 1 teaspoon lemon zest
- 1/2 teaspoon pure vanilla extract
- 1/8 teaspoon salt

For Shells:

Preheat oven to 280° F. Line a baking tray. Beat egg whites in a large mixing bowl with an electric beater for one minute. Add in granulated sugar. After another minute, add food coloring, lemon zest, and lemon juice. Beat until you can hold the bowl upside down and the egg mixture does not move, about 5 to 7 minutes.

Fold in ground almonds and powdered sugar with a flexible spatula. Scrape the sides of the bowl and move the mixture to the middle. Do this until everything is mixed well.

Pour the batter into a piping bag. Pipe into one-inch circles, leaving one inch between each. Should be around thirty circles.

Leave shells to dry for 30 minutes. Bake for 15 minutes, rotating the tray halfway through baking time.

When finished baking, let shells cool completely before attempting to remove them from the tray. If the shells are cracked, they will still be delicious.

For Buttercream Cream:

While macaron shells are drying, make buttercream.

Beat butter in a mixing bowl until fluffy. Add powdered sugar, heavy cream, lemon juice, lemon zest, vanilla extract, and salt and beat until well combined.

Assembly:

Turn macaron shells on their backs. Fill a piping bag with the buttercream and pipe small mounds of cream onto every other shell. Top with second shell.

About the Author

Harper Lin is a *USA TODAY* bestselling cozy mystery author.

When she's not reading or writing, she loves hiking, doing yoga, and hanging out with her family and friends.

For a complete list of her books by series, visit her website.

www.HarperLin.com